JUST A LITTLE
SECRET

NEW YORK TIMES BESTSELLING AUTHORS

Carly Phillips
Erika Wilde

**He's not just a bachelor up for auction …
He's her sexy birthday gift for the weekend.**

Georgia Brooks had no intention of bidding on a bachelor at the charity auction, but her sister has other ideas and gifts her with a *man* for her birthday weekend. But not just any man . . . Drew Daniels. A hot, gorgeous lawyer who makes her want to shed her good-girl image and learn all sorts of new and risqué things.

Attorney Drew Daniels is more than willing to introduce the beautiful Georgia to her naughtier side. Their weekend together is steamy and romantic . . . and it doesn't hurt that a rival of Drew's has his eye on Georgia, too. Stirring the other man's jealousy is a fun side benefit.

Their tryst should have been just about pleasure, but Drew finds he's attracted to more than Georgia's outer beauty and he wants to keep her as his own. When Drew suggests they continue their secret affair, Georgia is too smitten to say no. Even if her parents expect her to marry her lawyer father's right-hand man.

Georgia finds herself falling for Drew harder and faster than she could have imagined. Until she discovers he's forced to make a choice that has the potential to break her heart.

Chapter One

GEORGIA BROOKS STEPPED into the hotel ball-room, aware that tonight's Leadership in Law awards banquet was destined to be one long snooze fest, but her parents expected her to attend, and it wasn't in her personality to argue.

"Incoming! Georgia-seeking, heat missile arriving on the right," her younger sister said in a low, amused tone that only Georgia could hear.

She didn't know whether to laugh or scowl at Courtney's outrageous comment. Laugh, because the man making a beeline her way was so damn predicta-ble—and irritating. And scowl, because, well, Elliott Eastman was *so damn predictable. And irritating.*

Georgia had been prepared to deal with Elliott, knowing that as soon as she stepped into the room her father's protégé would notice and immediately seek her out. And she'd resigned herself to playing the good girl tonight because her father was being honored, and she didn't want to make a scene.

Sure enough, Elliott rushed over as if he'd had his eyes glued to the entrance just waiting for them to arrive so he could make his move.

Regardless of the fact that her father raved about the man who was fast becoming one of the top attorneys in his firm, his stalkerish behavior was creepy and unnerving. He'd just made junior partner, and Georgia knew Elliott had even higher aspirations…that included dating the boss's daughter.

"If it wasn't for Dad being up for the lifetime achievement award, I wouldn't have come tonight, and *he's* the reason," Georgia said, trying to tamp down her annoyance as Elliott neared. "I won't be able to enjoy myself with him hovering over me."

"I think he's trying to wear you down," Courtney said as they followed their parents further into the ballroom. "Be strong, Georgia. Don't let the fact that Mom and Dad are hoping that the two of you fall madly in love and produce a dozen babies together make you weak."

"Oh, my God, you are so gross." Georgia glared at her sister while desperately trying to wipe that image from her mind. "What are you? In high school?"

Courtney shrugged in that unapologetic way of hers. "You know I only speak the truth."

Unfortunately, she did.

In all honesty, Georgia envied her sister's outspoken attitude. Courtney was four years younger than Georgia, and she'd gone from being a precocious toddler to a rebellious, wild teenager. Even now, as a twenty-three-year-old adult, she had an impressive take-it-or-leave-it attitude that she expressed in all ways. From the pink highlights in her beach-wavy blonde hair to the gold ring in her nose and the boho chic dress she'd worn, Courtney flaunted her unconventional fashion style. In a room full of elegant cocktail gowns, including Georgia's classic little black dress, Courtney stood out. Most impressively, at least to Georgia, she didn't give a shit. At all.

Whereas Georgia had always been the more serious sister, the quintessential *good girl* who followed the rules, Courtney gleefully broke and defied them. Courtney said what was on her mind, sometimes without a filter, while Georgia kept things bottled up to prevent any friction. Her sibling was daring and fearless, the opposite of Georgia's more cautious and conservative nature. While she admired her sister's fearless attitude, Georgia *liked* herself just fine.

The problem only arose when it came to her parents. Then, being a people pleaser often came at her own expense. There had been one time Georgia had stood up for herself and she had no regrets. They'd wanted her to attend law school so she could work in her father's law firm, but she'd followed her passion and now had a degree in non-profit management. Her parents had been appalled and acted as if she'd caused a horrific scandal when *they'd* caused the awful family tension.

Their disapproval had nearly crippled Georgia with guilt, especially when her father's heart attack and triple bypass came shortly thereafter, but it was a decision that made her happy. She'd recently accepted a position with Future Fast Track, a non-profit dedicated to helping foster kids transition out of the system once they were of age. She honestly loved her job.

But despite that one act of rebellion, her parents still had certain expectations, and she was coming to realize that marrying Elliott and making him a part of their family was one of them. She was going to have to find her big girl panties once more because there was no way she could do as they wanted. The thought made her want to throw up.

Elliott finally reached them, and her father greeted his protégé with a broad smile. With Elliott's light-brown hair and hazel eyes, even Georgia could admit he was a good-looking man, but she felt no attraction toward him. At all. His egotistical air turned her off. Add in his twin habits of coming on too strong and kissing her father's ass, and she wanted nothing to do with him.

"Congratulations again, sir," Elliott said, shaking Roland Brooks' hand and holding on for too long. "I can't think of a more deserving attorney to receive the Leadership in Law lifetime achievement award."

"Thank you." Her father beamed, soaking up the attention and praise. "Keep up the good work, and you'll be the recipient yourself someday."

Elliott smiled wide, then turned his attention to Georgia's mother, Nina. "You look stunning tonight, Mrs. Brooks."

Suck up, Georgia thought, but swallowed back the retort.

Her mother blushed, and Georgia wondered if she could conjure her red cheeks at command. Nina Brooks *enjoyed* being fawned over by a younger man. "It's good to see you, Elliott. We must have you over to the house for dinner sometime soon."

He gave her a nod. "I would love that."

As Georgia expected, Elliott shifted his gaze, giving her a too-intimate stare that did nothing to stir any kind of sexual response inside her. "Of course, you look equally as lovely, Georgia. It's such a pleasure to see you, too." He lifted her hand and brushed his lips across her knuckles in a too-possessive gesture.

She did her best not to gag as the touch of his mouth made her skin crawl. If not for her parents watching the exchange—her father with pride and her mother with hope and anticipation—she would have yanked her hand back and possibly followed with a slap across his arrogant face.

At least in her dreams, that's what she would have done.

With no choice, she endured the unwanted attention and murmured a polite, "Nice to see you again, Elliott."

He moved on to say hello to Courtney, the warmth in his gaze cooling. They'd met before, but her sister didn't even pretend to be impressed by Elliott, and given her unconventional looks, he clearly felt the same way.

Courtney's gaze flicked over his designer suit. "Don't you look dapper tonight," she said in a cheeky tone.

His gaze narrowed as he obviously tried to decide if the old-fashioned term was a compliment or an insult. "Thank you," he replied...cautiously.

"Though you do have something on your nose," she added, and Elliot automatically rubbed two fingers over the tip before realizing what Courtney meant.

Georgia choked on a laugh at her sister calling him what he was. A brown-nosed, ass-kisser.

Georgia cleared her throat so her laugh couldn't escape while Elliott stiffened, his face flushing in embarrassment when he realized the subtle insinuation in Courtney's comment.

"You know, I'm sure there's a bottle of Corona at the bar with my name on it," Courtney said, clearly ready to separate herself, while Georgia knew she was stuck with Elliott.

"You know there are waiters walking around with glasses of champagne," their mother said, looking horrified at the thought of her daughter strolling about with a bottle of cheap, low-class beer at a high-society banquet.

Her sister wrinkled her pert nose. "Too refined for my tastes."

"Courtney, behave yourself," their father chided, though there was affection in his voice.

"Always, Daddy," Courtney said in a sweet tone, then walked over and kissed him on the cheek.

Courtney always got away with her outrageous be-havior, her father finding it cute while expecting

Georgia to be the epitome of the perfect society princess. It was so unfair, but she didn't blame her sister for their parents' attitude. Georgia adored Courtney and always would.

"I'll meet you all at our assigned table in a little bit." Courtney waved and strode off, many eyes in the room on her as she made her way through the crowd.

"Well." Her mother's gaze encompassed Georgia and Elliott. "Why don't you two go ahead and mingle. We'll see you at the table when it's time for dinner."

"That's a wonderful idea," Elliott said, obviously pleased her mother wanted them together.

Georgia resisted the urge to object to her mother's meddling suggestion. It would make her appear rude, and it was just easier to go with Elliott than deal with her mother's disapproving attitude for the rest of the evening.

Her parents moved in one direction, and Elliott lightly pressed his hand against the small of her back and guided her toward a younger group of people.

"Is your sister always so horrid?" he asked, clearly still peeved over Courtney's "nose" comment.

Georgia held back her smile, certain that Elliott wouldn't appreciate her finding the joke funny. "She's definitely her own person. She's an…acquired taste."

"Certainly not mine," he muttered beneath his breath, then seemed to visibly shake off his irritation. "So, let me introduce you around."

As if they were a couple. Ugh.

She'd already committed to this ruse and the last

thing she wanted was to cause a scene at an event honoring her father, so she followed Elliott's lead. She told herself it was just for the one night as he introduced her to a few of his colleagues…then promptly ignored her as he launched into a heated debate with one of the men in the group.

Georgia accepted a glass of champagne from a passing tray and made small, polite talk with the women in their circle before Elliott noticed someone else he wanted to talk to. And because he grabbed her hand each time he moved, and they were in a public setting, she followed along.

But she quickly grew bored of the shallow exchanges with strangers, and it didn't take her long to realize just how much Elliott and his giant-sized ego liked being the center of attention—continually bragging about becoming a junior partner at her father's firm, his latest win in court, or his superior performance on the golf course. Every conversation he had with another man felt like a dick measuring contest, and because Elliott seemed to boast the most, Georgia could only assume he was making up for *other* deficiencies. And she definitely didn't want to see his tiny penis, she mused.

The thought made her bite back a smile, though Georgia was sure her sister would agree with that theory. Which made her wonder where Courtney had gone.

She glanced around the room, trying to find her wayward sister, but couldn't see her anywhere. Just as she ended her search, Georgia locked gazes with a gorgeous man standing in his own circle of people a short distance away. A lively discussion seemed to be going on around him, but his attention was riveted on her, which made her wonder…how long had he been staring?

His gaze lingered and an immediate rush of heat pulsed through her body, settling in intimate places—and she couldn't glance away. He looked vaguely familiar, though she couldn't figure out why. She definitely would have remembered meeting an attractive, charismatic man like him.

He wore a dark-navy suit tailored to his tall, lean build and broad shoulders. His thick, dark-brown hair set off his masculine features, and those piercing green eyes that held hers made her think of sex and sin.

With him.

She breathed in a soft inhale of air, and as liquid desire trickled through her, she shifted restlessly in her heels.

As if he'd read her mind, his sexy lips quirked upward as he brought his glass of amber liquid to his mouth and took a sip. Her eyes followed the movement…and then he winked at her before returning his focus to the gentleman who was speaking.

His bold flirtation caused flutters of awareness to take up residence inside her. She couldn't remember ever being so drawn to a man before or so quickly aroused by just a look—not that she planned on doing anything about their brief but potent exchange.

A short while later, dinner was announced, and her sister suddenly appeared at her side, startling Georgia. As they walked together toward their assigned table, Elliott was thankfully still occupied speaking to a colleague.

She glanced at her sister. "Where have you been all this time?"

Courtney shrugged. "Around."

"Misbehaving?" *As their father had put it.*

"Always." Courtney grinned. "Actually, I was out on the balcony drinking my beer in peace and quiet, and scrolling through Tinder instead of mingling with all these stuffy suits and pretending I'm enjoying myself."

Georgia laughed at her sister's answer. Better than being dragged around by Elliott for the past hour and listening to him regurgitate the same conversation over and over again.

At their table, she sat between Elliott and her sister, mostly to keep them separated…and her sister well-behaved. Dinner was served and Elliott conversed with her father, giving her a chance to casually glance at the table next to theirs. Her gaze once again collided with the sexy man she'd seen earlier. He acknowledged her with a slight nod, then followed *that* up with a slow, seductive smile, and her entire body flushed with awareness.

She wasn't used to being the center of a man's attention, and she couldn't deny that she liked his interest.

"Hmm. Looks like you have an admirer," her sister said, catching sight of the exchange.

"What?" Georgia quickly averted her gaze and frowned at her sister. "No, I don't."

Courtney's eyes sparkled with mischief. "You know, if I were you, I'd ditch your boring date and see if that hot stranger wants to meet you in the bar downstairs for a drink…and whatever else you might be willing to put on the menu."

Georgia rolled her eyes. "Of course, you would." Unlike her sister, Georgia wasn't one for a random hookup with a stranger. No matter how hot and sexy he might be.

Courtney sighed dramatically. "When was the last time you got laid?"

Georgia nearly choked on the bite of filet mignon she'd been swallowing, then gaped at her sister, grateful she'd at least spoken in a low voice so no one else at the table had heard her. "Are you serious?"

"Of course I am." Courtney stabbed a glazed baby carrot with her fork. "If I had to guess, I'd say it was with Davis."

A relationship that had ended well over a year ago, and Georgia had no intention of admitting her sister was right.

"Your silence says it all," Courtney teased as she cut into her own tender filet. "You know, an orgasm with a real live dick would do you good. Your birthday is coming up in a few weeks. You should let your hair down, literally and figuratively, and treat yourself."

Georgia caught herself before she reached up to touch her upswept hair, then shook her head. "You are such a brat."

Courtney grinned. "And that's why *I* have the most fun."

Her sister wasn't wrong. The good girl/bad girl stereotype between them was real.

Chapter Two

O VER THE NEXT hour, Georgia finished eating dinner, sat through the awards ceremony, then the band began playing slow dancing music. Courtney slipped away to the bar to get a drink, their parents headed out to the dance floor, and Georgia quickly excused herself to use the ladies' room—before Elliott could wrangle her into joining them.

The last thing she wanted was to be trapped against him, her body pressed against his, and his hands wandering inappropriately.

After using the restroom and washing her hands, Georgia sat down in a comfortable chair in the lounge, buying herself time so she didn't have to deal with Elliott. She scrolled through social media—because she'd never be so daring as to have a Tinder account like her sister—then finally headed back to the ballroom.

The lights were dim, but she saw Elliott talking with a few other men and quickly headed in the opposite direction. The dessert table beckoned, and she walked over to the enticing selections. She picked up a small plate and perused the items on display, selecting two chocolate-covered strawberries. They were her favorite and she couldn't wait to taste them.

Picking up the bigger one of the two, she bit into the bottom, realizing too late they'd been injected with sweetened syrup. The berry was so plump and juicy that she had to suck on the fruit to catch it all with an unladylike slurp. Despite decorum, a little moan escaped her as she swallowed the abundance of nectar.

"I have to say, I've never been so envious of a strawberry before," a deep, sexy, masculine voice said from behind her.

Oh my God. She quickly pulled the fruit from her mouth and turned, flustered to find her admirer standing there grinning. Not only had he obviously seen and heard her display, but juice trickled at the corner of her mouth, adding to her mortification. With her plate in one hand and the strawberry in the other, she tried in vain to lick the sticky sweetness away.

"Here, let me help," he offered and reached out, skimming his thumb along her bottom lip to wipe away the juice. Then, holding her gaze, he brought his finger to his mouth and sucked off the taste, a naughty gleam in his light green eyes.

"Mmm." The low, rumbling sound he made was like an illicit caress in all her intimate spots. "So much sweeter than I thought."

Me or the strawberry, she wondered, and expelled a rush of breath as her cheeks heated.

The fire in his gaze answered her unspoken question. He was everything she wasn't used to in a man—

bold and daring in a room full of people and she couldn't help but be drawn to everything about him.

"Well, that was embarrassing," she managed to mutter, looking away as she set her plate of strawberries on a side table, then picked up a napkin to wipe her sticky fingers.

"Not for me." His voice held a teasing note. "I know *I'll* never look at a strawberry in quite the same way again." His huskily spoken words didn't help cool her body's reaction to him.

She swallowed back a groan and tried to put this conversation on a less provocative track, which was difficult when just the sound of this man's voice was a seduction in and of itself.

"Well, uh, thank you for your help." She put on her most polite smile before remembering her manners. "I'm Georgia Brooks, by the way."

"Happy to be of assistance, *Georgia*." Even the way he drawled her name sent delicious shivers down her spine. "I'm assuming you're Roland Brooks' daughter since I saw you sitting at his table?"

"Yes." Now that he was so close, she studied his gorgeous face, and that earlier feeling of familiarity returned, along with a jolt of recognition. "And you're Drew Daniels."

His brows rose in surprise. "Does my reputation precede me?"

She laughed and shook her head. "I thought you looked familiar when I first saw you earlier. I recognized you from the photos for the upcoming bachelor auction. I work for Future Fast Track, and we just received the booklets for the charity event. Your picture and profile are inside."

He cringed and pushed his hands into the front pockets of his slacks. "Ah, yes, I got roped into that event. Not my thing, but I'm all about supporting a good cause. Not to mention, my sister-in-law, Chloe, twisted my arm. Aurora is her sister."

Georgia nodded with a smile. She liked Aurora, her boss and founder of Future Fast Track, and enjoyed working for her non-profit. And Georgia had met Chloe Kingston Daniels a few times when she'd stopped in to have lunch with Aurora. Chloe was married to Beck, one of Drew's brothers. Their other brother, Tripp—a pediatrician—was also a bachelor up for auction for the charity.

Drew glanced around the general area, then his gaze came back to her. "So, where did your boyfriend disappear to?"

She frowned. "Boyfriend?" She played dumb because she'd been tugged around by Elliott all evening, but no way did she want this man to think she was taken.

"Elliott Eastman," he clarified. "The man you've been with for most of the evening. He seems quite...possessive of you, so I assumed he's your boyfriend."

"God, no," she blurted out. "We're just, uh, friends."

"Friends?" he repeated with a slight tip to his head.

She lifted her shoulders in a small shrug. "Okay, even that's a gracious word for what we are."

He laughed, the sound low and husky and very pleased. "Good to know. In that case, would you like to dance, Ms. Brooks?"

He'd asked just as the current song segued into a slower ballad. While she'd managed to avoid dancing with Elliott, the thought being up close and personal with Drew was a whole different matter.

"I would love to," she said, accepting the hand he offered and allowing him to lead her to the dance area.

As soon as they were on the parquet flooring, he lifted her hand and guided her into a slow twirl that made her little black dress flare around her legs. The spin ended with him pulling her close, her body flush against his.

He made the maneuver feel so effortless, and she glanced up at him with a smile. "Look at you, breaking out those smooth dance moves."

He chuckled, placing his free hand low on her spine to keep her in place. "I'm doing what I can to impress you."

She was secretly delighted that he wanted to get her attention. "You're doing an excellent job," she said, still breathless from the move.

Only the thin silk material of her dress separated her skin from his, and her nerve endings sizzled and sparked at the faint brush of his fingertips against her lower back. She had the shameless urge to arch into his body and invite him to keep exploring, moving downward until his big, strong hand cupped her rear end perfectly…but she was disappointed.

He was the consummate gentleman if she didn't count the sinful gleam in his eyes or the way he shifted their bodies so his hard, muscular thighs rubbed enticingly against hers. Every inch of him was a heady combination of masculinity and grace, and the scent of his expensive cologne made her want to bury her face in his neck and breathe him in.

"Speaking of being impressed," she said, trying to distract herself from her attraction to this man. "Congratulations on receiving the Lawyers of Distinction Award tonight."

"Thank you," he replied, no elaborating or bragging.

It had been a pleasure watching Drew during the awards ceremony. She'd admired the confident way he'd walked on stage to accept his crystal statue and his thoughtful speech about what a huge privilege it was to be nominated with so many other outstanding attorneys. He seemed genuinely honored and grateful for the recognition, and a touch humble, as well.

Though Elliott hadn't been up for the award, she hadn't missed his disgruntled expression or how he'd scoffed under his breath during Drew's speech. She chalked it up to Elliott being jealous and feeling less than in light of Drew's accomplishment.

"So, you work for Future Fast Track," Drew said, shifting the focus off himself and onto her. "I take it you had no desire to follow in your father's footsteps and work at his law firm?"

"No." She shook her head, all too aware of his gaze on her lips. "I know my parents would have preferred that career choice, but it's just not something I'm passionate about."

His eyes darkened at her choice of words. "Go on, Georgia. Tell me more about what you *are* passionate about."

She licked her dry lips. "I love working for a non-profit and doing what I can to make a difference in a foster kid's life. It's hard enough becoming a young adult, but to age out of the system, they need help the state doesn't provide."

Warmth filled his gaze. "You like giving back to those less fortunate."

"I do," she admitted, surprised by how easy it was to open up and talk to Drew, a man she'd just met. "I know there's plenty of opportunity to do that in law, but I'm not cut out for the stress and pressure of the profession. At the end of the day, I just want to feel good about helping others build a better life for themselves."

"That's admirable," he said with a charming smile.

"Thank you." It was the first time someone had acknowledged what she did in a positive manner—unlike her parents, who dismissed her work as a passing phase, which hurt. "That's...nice to hear." She heard the gratitude in her voice, and she glanced away from Drew's intense gaze.

She didn't want to reveal so much to a man she'd

just met. He was perceptive enough as it was. But she couldn't deny there was a warmth and ease with Drew, and she found their connection both exhilarating and unnerving. She'd never felt so relaxed and comfortable with a man so quickly.

He gently touched her chin with his thumb and forefinger, startling her as he rubbed his thumb over a faint, fine scar on the left side.

"What happened here?" he asked, his voice a low, curious murmur as his fingertip brushed across her skin.

The barely-there scar was such an odd thing to notice, let alone comment on, which told her just how observant he was. He paid attention to even the smallest of details instead of talking about himself all the time.

"When I was six, I tripped and fell face-first against the corner of a coffee table, split my chin open, and needed stitches." A smile tipped the corner of her mouth where he was still touching, both at the memory and in appreciation of his attention.

"And you still have a very faint scar," he mused, seemingly charmed by that slight flaw she'd all but forgotten about.

"My mother wanted me to see a plastic surgeon," she admitted. "As a kid, I freaked out whenever she mentioned it because of how painful the shot and stitches had been. No way did I want surgery on it. Then, as I grew older, it became a little act of rebellion not to have it removed."

Chuckling, he returned his hand to her lower back. "An act of rebellion?" He raised an inquisitive brow.

"Yeah," she acknowledged and added, "Though it doesn't happen very often."

He studied her for a long moment. "Just when it's over something that really matters to you."

There it was again, that intuitive understanding. "You need to stop getting into my head," she said, though she was smiling.

"I can't help myself." He leaned his head closer, until his lips were near her ear. "I find you *very* intriguing, Georgia Brooks."

She shivered and exhaled a deep breath, and when he pulled back and she saw the genuine attraction in his gaze, she allowed herself to be bolder than usual. "I could say the same for you."

The song came to an end, and the warm palm at her back tightened as if he wasn't quite ready to let her go just yet, even though the band announced they were taking a short break. "In that case, how would you like to—"

"Georgia!"

The demanding sound of Elliott calling her name jarred her out of the moment and cut off whatever Drew had been about to say.

He *slowly* released her and took a step back. Losing his touch was the last thing she wanted and frustration at Elliott's persistence flared inside her.

"I've been looking all over for you," Elliott said, sounding annoyed as he reached the two of them.

Georgia forced herself to remain calm and shifted her gaze to Elliott, who openly glared at Drew. "I was just enjoying a dance with Drew, who I assume you know?"

Elliott's lips thinned. "Yes, I know who Drew is."

Drew seemed unfazed by the other man's attitude. "Good to see you, Eastman," he said pleasantly.

Elliott didn't return the sentiment, and instead ignored Drew completely. "Your parents are asking me where you've disappeared to."

"I'm an *adult*, Elliott," she said, irritated that he was questioning her whereabouts. "I don't need my parents' permission to do *anything*. Or yours, either, for that matter."

Drew stood by, silently amused, if his raised lips were anything to go by.

Anger flashed in Elliott's eyes. He clearly didn't appreciate being chastised in public, but he'd brought it on himself by acting as though he had a right to dictate her actions.

"It's time to go back to our table," Elliott said.

She crossed her arms over her chest and stood her ground. "I'm not done talking to Drew, so I'd appreciate it if you'd give us some privacy, please."

Elliott hesitated, obviously wanting to argue, but after an uncomfortable moment, he whirled around and strode back to the table. She'd like to think that was the end of things, but when he sat back down, he chose a chair with a clear view of her and Drew.

Ignoring Elliott's stare, she refocused her attention

on the man in front of her. Drew appeared calm and composed despite Elliott's odd animosity toward him.

"I'm so sorry about that. I don't know what's gotten into him." Elliott could be possessive, but his reaction to Drew was over the top, even for him.

"There's no telling," he said wryly—but the mischievous glimmer in his eyes told her he knew exactly why Elliott had overreacted so badly.

Drew didn't offer an explanation, and she tried to backtrack their conversation. "So, you were about to ask me something before Elliott interrupted us?"

"It was nothing," he said, giving her a slight smile, one at odds with the warmth he'd exhibited earlier. "It was a pleasure meeting you, Georgia. I suppose I'll see you at the Future Fast Track charity event?"

That magical moment between them was gone, and she couldn't stem the disappointment that filled her. "Yes, I'll be there."

He inclined his head, their former intimacy replaced by a more reserved demeanor. Now she couldn't imagine what had gotten into *him*.

"Have a good night," he said much too cordially, then turned and walked away.

Georgia watched him go, her chest tight, feeling as though something special had just slipped through her fingers. Which was ridiculous considering she barely knew the man. But it was clear that Drew's shift in demeanor was directly related to Elliott's interruption. She just didn't understand *why*.

With a sigh, she headed back to their table to gath-

CARLY PHILLIPS & ERIKA WILDE

er her things, more than ready to leave. The evening had been winding down anyway, and she wanted to go home.

Elliott rushed up to her, a deep scowl on his flushed face. "You need to keep your distance from Drew Daniels," he demanded.

She stopped short and stared. "Excuse me?" she asked, taking offense to him ordering her around.

"Look, Georgia, the guy is smooth, I'll give him that. But he isn't what he seems. He's arrogant and cocky and more flash than substance. Not to mention, he uses people for his own gain."

She refrained, just barely, from pointing out that Elliott had just described himself. How did her father not see this pretentious side to him?

"What do you have against Drew?" she asked instead.

A look of surprise crossed his face, his eyes wide and his mouth parted, but he remained silent, his reaction telling her she was on point. Elliott was jealous of Drew, and it wasn't just about finding Georgia with the man. He'd begun pouting when Drew had received his award.

Elliott quickly recovered. "What do I have against him? Besides his lack of ethics and conceit?"

Drew hadn't come across as being either of those things. In fact, he'd had every chance to bad mouth Elliott once he'd left them alone, but he hadn't said a word—yet here *Elliott* was, trying to warn her off Drew.

She refused to get into a debate or argument with him. Instead, Georgia walked around Elliott to their table, grabbed her purse, and started for the exit.

She pulled out her phone and texted her mother and sister to let them know she was leaving. She didn't want them to wait or worry about her. Then she pulled up her Uber app.

"Where are you going?" Elliott asked.

Had he really followed her? "Home," she replied curtly. "I'm tired." And he'd completely ruined her evening.

"Let me at least drive you," he insisted.

She shuddered at the thought, knowing a ride from him would probably come with other expectations. "No, I'm good, and I'd like to be alone."

He exhaled a frustrated breath but walked her out to the valet area. Thankfully, he didn't pressure her any further. He stood by until she was safely inside her ride before striding back into the hotel.

The driver pulled away from the curb, and she slumped in her seat, wishing she was going home with Drew instead of heading to her apartment alone. But that thought was destined to be nothing more than a fantasy. Because not only had Drew left her on the dance floor—despite what she'd thought was a sizzling attraction—but good, responsible girls like Georgia didn't indulge in one-night stands.

Chapter Three

DREW WATCHED HIS brother, Tripp, make the final winning shot into the basketball hoop and groaned in annoyance—mostly at himself and his inability to focus on the game. He'd always had a competitive streak, especially when it came to his brothers, and he hated to lose. It also didn't happen very often.

Tripp looked much too pleased with himself as he jogged off to the sidelines to retrieve the basketball, then dribbled it back toward where Drew was heading for the bench seats.

They played at an indoor court at their gym in the city. With Tripp having just turned thirty-six, and Drew thirty-four, they were both in great shape and hit the gym regularly to keep fit. Every once in a while, their youngest brother, Beck, graced them with his presence, as well.

Drew sat down and lifted the hem of his T-shirt to wipe the sweat off his face just as Tripp joined him.

"You can't play worth a shit today," his brother said, still gloating a bit. "What has you so distracted? A case you're working on?"

That was the logical assumption since Drew handled a lot of high-profile mergers and acquisitions clients at McKenzie Goodwin. Since making partner almost a year ago, his workload had definitely increased, but that wasn't the reason for his head not being in the game today.

"Would you believe me if I told you it was a woman?" he admitted.

"Well, now you've got my attention." Tripp sat down, placed the ball on the ground, then tossed Drew one of the two bottled waters next to him. "I didn't even know you were seeing anyone."

"I'm not," he said, cracking open the top before taking a long drink of the cool liquid, which felt great going down his dry throat. "I met her at the awards dinner last night."

Tripp smirked. "I can't remember the last time you got hung up on a one-night stand."

Drew shook his head and corrected his brother. "I didn't sleep with her."

Tripp's dark brows rose over his green eyes as he gulped his own water. When he was done, he said, "And now I'm even more intrigued, so spill."

When Drew agreed to meet Tripp at the gym for a game of one-on-one—which didn't happen often with both of their crazy schedules—he hadn't intended on discussing his encounter with Georgia. But considering she was occupying too much of his brain power, he decided to talk about the evening with his brother to hopefully clear his head.

He glanced at Tripp. "Do you remember Elliott Eastman, the dick colleague I told you about that's always resented my success?"

Tripp didn't have to think long. "Oh, yeah...the one who nearly had an aneurysm when you bagged the eight-billion-dollar merger between Gould Logistics and Capstone, over him?"

Drew nodded, even though their rivalry encompassed so much more than that one client. It went back to their law school years, but acquiring that huge corporation hadn't helped matters. The contention between the two of them had always been instigated by Elliott, who never missed an opportunity to belittle Drew, which was ironic since Drew came out on top more often than not.

"Ahh, so you do listen when I talk to you," Drew said to Tripp, then finished off his water.

His brother chuckled. "Sometimes. But in this case, it's hard to forget the accomplishment that put you on the fast track to making partner. So, what about Elliott Eastman?"

Drew leaned forward and braced his forearms on his knees. "He was there last night with a woman I assumed was his date." His mind went back to the first moment he'd seen Georgia accompanying Elliott as he made the rounds during cocktail hour. Drew's first thought had been, *what was a beauty like her doing with a schmuck like Elliott?*

And she *was* beautiful. He'd been captivated by her pretty face with delicate features and expressive blue eyes, made more prominent with her blonde hair swept into some kind of stylish updo. She'd worn a modest black cocktail dress, but there was no missing her full breasts, curvy hips, and long, slender legs that inspired all sorts of dirty thoughts.

So when he'd seen her alone at the dessert table, Drew figured there was no harm in talking to her—and if their interaction irritated Eastman, he'd count it as a bonus. He thought she'd be nothing more than a flighty piece of arm candy or a spoiled socialite, but quickly realized how wrong that presumption had been.

"Hey, where'd you go?" his brother asked, dragging Drew's thoughts away from Georgia.

So much for talking about her to get his mind back on track.

He gave his head a shake. "I'll admit, I might have approached her when she was alone for the sole purpose of annoying the douchebag, and I'd only intended to flirt with her a bit. But then she told me that Elliott wasn't her boyfriend, so I asked her to dance."

In the short twenty minutes he'd been in Georgia Brooks' presence, he'd been introduced to a sophisticated woman who came across as strong, intelligent, and mature. Yet, there had been a few times when she'd also given him a look into underlying self-doubts that surprised him. He would have missed those nuances had he not been paying such close attention to the emotion in her eyes, her revealing expression, and her soft voice.

He wasn't lying when he said she intrigued him. More than was probably wise.

"So, you danced, and what happened?" Tripp prompted, making Drew realize that he'd let his mind wander. *Again.*

He glanced at his brother. "There was a genuine connection and attraction between us, which I wasn't expecting at all. I mean, I haven't felt that kind of chemistry with a woman since…Angie."

"Wow," Tripp said, his eyes widening in surprise. "It's only taken what, three years for you to get past her betrayal?"

Drew shrugged. "I've been over Angie since the day I found out she was having an affair with someone else."

Tripp arched a disbelieving brow, which Drew ignored. He was definitely over Angie, but he wasn't about to admit to his brother that being burned by her *had* put his guard up with women in general, which resulted in a lot of one-night stands to avoid anything deeper.

His busy career—which entailed long days and sometimes even longer nights—had also kept him from seriously dating anyone since his ex, especially when he remembered the excuse Angie had given him for sleeping with another man. She'd complained that Drew never had any time for her, and she needed more than he was ready or willing to give. Which, at the time, had been true.

However, Angie's issues with him had been a shitty excuse to have an affair, and there was no justification for what she'd done. She should have broken things off *before* riding another man's dick, and her cheating was a reminder to Drew that his heavy caseload and schedule, especially now that he was a partner, wasn't conducive to starting a relationship. Never mind giving it the time and attention it needed to thrive.

"Tell me you at least asked her out since you obviously can't stop thinking about her," Tripp said, shaking him out of his deeper thoughts. For yet a third time.

"I almost did," Drew said, absently crunching the empty plastic bottle in his hand. "But Elliott interrupted us, and the more I thought about it, I realized that getting involved with her would just be stupid." *So he'd turned cold on her and let her go*, he thought with a grimace at the memory.

"Why?" Tripp asked, frowning. "You said she's not dating Elliott."

Drew rubbed a hand along the back of his neck. "No, she's not, but her father, Roland Brooks, is Elliott's boss, and their firm is a direct competitor to McKenzie Goodwin."

Tripp winced as understanding dawned. "Oh, yeah, that might be a conflict of interest."

"Also, about a week ago, my boss called me into his office," Drew went on. "Our firm just signed a big European client, and the senior partners offered me

31

the chance to head the legal team and represent the corporation in all their negotiations. It's a huge coup, but it would mean a lot of traveling to Europe."

Tripp's brows rose. "That's fantastic."

"But not exactly conducive to giving time and attention to a new relationship." He sighed heavily. "And honestly, it's difficult to say no to that kind of career opportunity, which will require a lot of my focus and extremely long hours, especially during all the initial formalities."

His brother nodded in understanding. "I totally get it. I felt the same way when I was just starting out as a pediatrician. Kind of like keeping your nose to the grindstone until you get where you want to be in your career."

"Exactly." Which was why Drew wasn't looking to get attached to anyone right now.

As much as he hated to admit it, it was probably for the best that Elliott had interrupted them right when he'd been about to ask Georgia if she'd like to join him for dinner sometime. The other man's untimely intrusion had snapped Drew out of his infatuation and made him realize just how complicated dating Georgia could get.

But knowing it was the right thing to do didn't mean he lacked regrets about walking away from her last night. He was disappointed they wouldn't get the chance to get to know one another better, but the last thing he'd ever want to do was put Georgia in the middle of his rivalry with Elliott. Even if it was, for the most part, one-sided.

Another group of guys came in to use the basket-ball court, and Drew and Tripp stood up, gathered their things, and strode toward the locker room.

"By the way, Georgia works for Aurora's non-profit," Drew said, tossing their empty water bottles into the recycling bin. "She recognized me from the bachelor auction brochure."

"Small world," Tripp commented, since their sis-ter-in-law, Chloe, was Aurora's sister. "So, I assume Georgia will be at the charity auction?"

The thought of seeing her again made his pulse race a bit faster, even though nothing could come of it. "Yes. More as a representative for Future Fast Track than a guest, I'm assuming."

"I'm not thrilled that we got suckered into being a part of the auction," Tripp grumbled, not for the first time.

"I'm right there with you," Drew agreed as they walked into the men's locker room. "But it's kind of hard to say no when Chloe bats her lashes and says it's all for charity, and Beck made it clear we should say yes because he didn't want to have to kick our asses for hurting his wife's feelings if we refused."

"It's not fucking fair that Beck is off the hook," Tripp said, sounding peeved.

Drew opened his locker. "Well, I suppose that's one perk of being married."

"That, and getting laid regularly," Tripp joked.

"Yeah, he's a lucky bastard," Drew added with a

laugh as he pulled his sweaty shirt off and replaced it with a dry one to wear home. "I already let my boss know that I'm participating in the auction and that at some point I'd need a weekend off. I just need to make the timing work."

The agreement they'd signed once they'd committed to the auction stipulated that they'd be required to spend a Friday evening through Sunday morning with whoever won them. Drew wasn't sure how he felt about that—it would either be a good thing, or a bad thing, depending on who won the bid and what their weekend together entailed.

"Is getting a weekend off going to be a problem for you?" Tripp changed out of his T-shirt as well and tossed the sweaty one into his gym bag. "I know you've been working hellacious hours lately."

"At the moment, it shouldn't be an issue. I just wrapped up the multi-billion-dollar merger I've been working on for the past eight months. Of course I've got a few other acquisitions on my plate and the European offer from the senior partners to think about, but nothing pressing for the next few weeks. I'll make it work. How about you?"

"I'll make sure I'm not on call that weekend," Tripp said.

As a pediatrician, Tripp worked in a small family practice with two other physicians who were partners together in the medical group. It worked well for them in terms of always having someone on call for the evenings and weekends.

They grabbed their car keys, cell phones, and gym bags and headed out to the parking garage. On the way, Tripp's phone chirped, and he checked the text message that came through. The cocky grin that curved his lips told Drew that the message wasn't work-related.

"What are you smirking about?" he asked his brother, certain it had to do with a woman. "Are you holding out on me after giving me shit about my non-existent sex life?"

"Maybe." Tripp looked way too enthusiastic as he replied to the text, then stopped at his car.

Drew paused beside his brother, curious to know what, or who, had just lifted his brother's mood.

"I kind of hooked up with an old flame Friday night," Tripp admitted.

Drew couldn't hide his surprise. "Julia?" It was the only woman Drew could think of since she was Tripp's most recent ex.

"No." His brother grimaced at the mention of her name and shook his head. "It's not anyone you would know. Just someone I had a friends-with-benefits arrangement with while I was in med school."

Tripp didn't offer anything more, clearly not ready to share any details, so Drew let it go. Instead, he said, "Well, I guess I'll see you at the auction next week-end."

Tripp nodded.

After saying goodbye, they went their separate ways. As Drew drove to his apartment, his mind drifted back to Georgia. A dozen "what ifs" trailed through his head as he thought about the chemistry and attraction that had been so potent between them the night before.

What if he did ask her out on a date? What if that date led to a hot, provocative kiss? What if that kiss led to them tearing each other's clothes off and ended up with her in his bed, moaning beneath him as he drove into her soft body? And what if—

He abruptly shut down those arousing scenarios because it wasn't going to happen. It *couldn't* happen. There was too much conflict and history with Elliott, and Elliott worked for Georgia's father's firm. Nothing about an affair with her would end well.

The only thing he could hope was that maybe a weekend with the random woman who won him at the auction would finally help curtail his interest in Georgia Brooks.

GEORGIA TAPED UP the last of the boxes that needed to be delivered to the Meridian Hotel in the city for the charity event coming up that weekend. Most of the basic set-up of the ballroom and tables was being handled by Lauren and Skye, the hotel's event coordinators, but the swag bags, props, banners from corporate sponsors and other branded décor had been gathering in Future Fast Track's offices over the past few months and needed to be assembled on-site.

Once all the items finally arrived at the hotel via a delivery service tomorrow, she and Billie—Aurora's office manager—along with the temporary staff they'd hired to help organize and arrange everything, would have three days to prepare for the gala. It would be a time-consuming task, but Georgia was excited to see their ideas and vision for the event finally come together.

Aurora walked—or rather, waddled, since she was seven months pregnant—into the office where they'd been storing things and added a stack of glossy poster boards with details about the silent auction, the bachelor auction, and information on the non-profit, on top of the pile of boxes. Her blonde hair was pulled back into a high ponytail, and she was dressed casually in dark-gray leggings and a pink blouse that conformed to her cute baby bump since they knew they'd be packing things up for the gala and she needed to be comfortable.

Aurora exhaled a tired sigh, though she was smiling with pride, obviously satisfied with how the charity event was turning out. "I can't believe this is all finally coming together," she said, groaning as she pressed a hand to her lower back while stretching her spine. "I think we're just about done here at the office."

"I think *you're* done," Georgia pointed out as she set the tape dispenser on a box. "You're putting in long days, and you've got to be exhausted."

"I agree," Billie said, adjusting her black-framed glasses on the bridge of her nose. With her pink hair and light-blue eyes, she reminded Georgia a bit of her sister, Courtney. "It's after seven, and I'm surprised that Nick hasn't charged in here to drag you home yet."

Aurora grinned impishly. "He's been texting me, but I told him I really needed to see this through, and he understands how important this event is to me. But he did make my favorite chicken tortilla soup for dinner and promised me a foot rub after I get home and Leah has gone to bed. I can't wait."

Even though Georgia had worn tennis shoes today, the soles of her own feet ached, too, from all the hustling they'd done over the past ten hours. "That sounds like heaven."

"Oh, it will be," Aurora said, and laughed.

Despite how the first seventeen years of Aurora's life had started out—being bounced from various foster homes, then being pregnant and homeless before her true family found her—she was always so optimistic and happy. And now she had the perfect little family and a husband that absolutely adored her.

Georgia found it hard not to be a bit envious of that kind of fairy tale life and relationship. She definitely wanted that for herself—with a man she chose on her own and not one hand-picked by her parents.

"So, let's all call it a night," Aurora said, breaking into Georgia's thoughts. "The delivery guys will be here first thing in the morning to pick up everything and take it to the hotel, and then we can get started setting up the ballroom."

"*We*, as in me and Billie and the staff," Georgia pointed out. "*You* are going to sit with your feet up and delegate what you want where."

Aurora rolled her eyes. "We'll see."

As soon as Aurora turned around and walked out of the room, Georgia exchanged a conspiratorial look with Billie so that they were both on the same page about making sure Aurora didn't overexert herself over the next few days.

After shutting down the office, the three of them rode the elevator to the parking garage. Aurora slipped into the hired town car waiting for her, while Georgia and Billie headed to their respective vehicles. Georgia just barely turned out of the structure and onto the main street when her cell phone rang.

The number came up on her car's display, and she groaned when she saw that it was her mother. She'd already called Georgia a few times today, leaving messages to the effect of *I have something I need to discuss with you.*

Judging by the terse tone of her mother's voice, she was annoyed over something, and since the call wasn't urgent, and Georgia had been going non-stop all day, she'd let all her calls go to voice mail and sent her mother a quick, *I'm busy and I'll call you later* text.

But there was no avoiding Nina Brooks for long, so Georgia picked up the call through her car's Bluetooth feature. "Hello, Mother," she said, trying not to sound as tired as she felt as she drove toward her apartment.

"*Finally*, you answered my call," Nina said dramatically.

Georgia rolled her eyes. "I've had a full day at the office, and I'm just now headed home for the night."

Her mother made a disapproving clucking sound. "You work for a non-profit organization. How difficult and busy can your days really be?"

"Very," Georgia said, hating how her mother minimized her career. "The charity event is this weekend, and we're getting everything set up."

"Oh, right. Aren't there people to do that for you?"

Georgia refrained, just barely, from smacking her head on the steering wheel in frustration. "Mom, *I'm* the 'people.' I'm a paid employee, and this is my job." She exhaled a deep, calming breath and got to the point of the call. "What did you need to discuss with me?"

"Well, I happened to come across some photos that the Leadership in Law website posted of the awards banquet," she said in a huff. "Why were you dancing with another man?"

Her mother's question, asked in that disapproving tone of hers, was the last thing she'd been expecting to hear—and the memory of Drew's warm, firm body pressed so intimately against hers flooded her mind. "Because he *asked* me to dance?"

"You were there with Elliott," her mother chastised Georgia. "I can't imagine how humiliated you made him feel, seeing you with another man when you were his date for the evening."

Georgia gripped the steering wheel tighter in her hands. "I wasn't Elliott's date. I came to the banquet solo, and you and Dad pushed me off on him. I'm sorry if you or Elliott thought differently. He's not my type at all."

"How do you know that?" her mother argued, ignoring all the other points Georgia just made. "You haven't given him a real chance. He's called you a few times since the banquet to take you to dinner, and you keep turning him down."

The fact that her mother was aware of Elliott's attempts to ask her out shocked Georgia. "How do you even know that?"

"Elliott mentioned it to your father, and your father told me."

Of course. Georgia turned on the side street leading to her building. "I keep turning Elliott down because I don't want to date him."

The interior of Georgia's car went silent for long, drawn-out seconds. Her stomach twisted in knots because she knew what was coming, and she tried to brace herself for the guilt her mother was about to heap on her conscience.

"Georgia," she began with feigned patience. "We let you take a job at a non-profit when your father and I always hoped you'd follow in his footsteps and become a lawyer. Since that's clearly not going to happen, the least you could do is open yourself up to the idea of someone like Elliott, who is a successful attorney in your father's firm and is showing incredible potential to take his place someday."

Georgia's entire mind was still stuck on "we *let* you take a job at a non-profit," when in truth, she'd stood up for herself and hadn't given them a choice. Yes, it had caused contention, but the fact that her mother was now twisting things around for her own purposes grated on Georgia's nerves. "Mom—"

"I'm not finished, Georgia," Nina said, cutting her off. "And since it's so hard to get ahold of you these days because you're so *busy*, let me have my say."

Georgia had never back-talked to either of her parents, mostly out of respect for an authoritative figure, and she had to swallow back the very strong urge to argue now. "Go on, Mother. I'm listening."

"You know your father's health is…fragile," she said, referencing the heart attack and triple bypass he'd gone through shortly after Georgia had made her career decisions, which only compounded her guilt. "He'll be retiring in the next few years, and he'd always hoped to leave the firm in the family, like his father and grandfather before him. Your father and I really do think you and Elliott would be a good match, so I don't understand why you're being so stubborn about the possibility."

Her head now pounding with tension, Georgia parked her car in her assigned slot and rested her head on the steering wheel. She hated the expectations that always seemed to hang over her as the oldest child. "The fact that you want me to marry Elliott for business reasons is an antiquated concept. You realize that, don't you?"

"We just want you to give him a chance," her mother said, her tone more subdued now. "Is that so much to ask? Just…think about it."

"Fine, I'll think about it," Georgia agreed, just to appease her mother and get her off the phone more quickly, but she knew her feelings regarding Elliott wouldn't change.

At some point, when her life wasn't so insanely busy, she needed to sit her parents down and make it clear that she had no interest in Elliott and never would. That her life was her own and she wouldn't force herself to like or God forbid, *marry* someone for the sake of saving the family business. Which didn't need saving at all. The firm would survive without a Brooks at the helm.

The call ended, and Georgia dragged herself up to her apartment. Once inside, she kicked off her shoes and then poured herself a glass of wine. Sitting on the couch, she put her feet up, took a nice long drink, and rested her head against the sofa cushion.

She closed her eyes, trying to relax, unwind, and de-stress after her long day and the call with her mother, and instead thought about the man who did make her feel…all sorts of things. Just the image of Drew and his gorgeous face made her body heat with arousal, her breasts tighten against her T-shirt, and her core pulse and ache with desire.

She'd given her battery-operated boyfriend quite a

workout since their encounter, while imagining what it would be like to lose all control with a purely masculine man like him, and make up for all the lackluster sex she'd had in the past.

A quiet little groan slipped past her lips as she thought about breaking out of her good girl comfort zone and doing something wild and scandalous for once in her life. It was an exhilarating thought, to do something just for herself...like have a torrid affair with Drew.

Too bad that would only happen in her mind. Because she couldn't forget that Drew had walked away from her and the possibility of something more. And she wasn't the kind of woman who chased a man who didn't want her in return.

Chapter Four

"WHERE DID TRIPP disappear to?" Drew asked, glancing around the crowded ballroom for his brother at the Future Fast Track charity event. "The bachelor auction is about to start."

"He probably slipped out the nearest exit," his younger brother, Beck, said with a smirk. "I know that's where I would have gone by now."

His beautiful wife, Chloe—dressed in a stunning gold-hued gown—lightly jabbed Beck in the side with her elbow. "Stop trying to cause trouble," she said, pursing her lips at her husband. "It was hard enough to wrangle your brothers into agreeing to this bachelor auction without you provoking them right before they need to get up on the stage."

Beck put his arm around her waist, pulled her close to his side, and pressed a kiss to her temple. "Sorry," he said, not sounding contrite at all.

Drew finished off the last of his bourbon and set the empty glass on a passing tray, his narrowed gaze still searching the area for his wayward brother. "I swear, I will kick his ass all the way to New Jersey if he somehow managed to get out of this while I'm being sold off like a prime piece of cattle."

Beck chuckled, then quickly cleared his throat when Chloe shot him a chastising look before glancing back at Drew. "Don't worry. I saw him at the bar talking to Skye." She pointed toward the corner of the room.

"Skye?" Drew craned his neck in that direction, and sure enough, he spotted Tripp standing with a pretty blonde woman that he didn't recognize, but Chloe clearly knew. "Do I know her?"

His sister-in-law shook her head. "She's a fairly new event coordinator for the Meridian Hotel and works with Jade and Lauren. I've seen him speaking to her a few times tonight."

Huh. Drew found that bit of information interesting. Especially since he could see Tripp's charming grin and knew that he was flirting with the other woman. First, a hookup with an old flame, and now trying to win over another female before being auctioned off to someone else. His brother was a very busy man with the ladies, lately.

He meant to return his attention back to Chloe and Beck, but a different blonde caught his gaze, and not for the first time that evening. Georgia seemed to always be on the opposite side of the room. Granted, he knew she was busy helping to make sure the event ran smoothly, but it was as though she was strategically trying to avoid him. Not that he could blame her. He'd given her no reason to seek him out after the abrupt way he'd ended things the last time he'd seen her.

But that didn't stop him from watching her work the room, along with Aurora and a pink-haired woman, all three smiling and talking to various guests and networking for the non-profit. Tonight, Georgia had worn her hair down in soft, loose curls, and was wearing a beaded black gown that shimmered in the light and accentuated her curves every time she moved.

He felt that familiar stirring of desire and had to resist the urge to approach her and apologize for his behavior that night at the banquet. To just say screw it and fucking kiss her like he wanted to do, then and now. But it really wasn't the time or the place, and it wouldn't change the fact that she was off-limits.

He forced his gaze back to his brother and Chloe, who was texting on her cell phone with an intent look on her face.

"Is everything okay?" Drew asked.

Beck nodded. "Yeah, she's just checking in with the sitter to see how Whitney is doing."

Whitney…their three-year-old daughter, named after their sister, and Tripp's twin. At one time, her name would have made Drew's chest tighten with grief as it had for years after she'd died of leukemia at the age of sixteen. Everyone in the family had dealt with her illness and subsequent death in different ways, all of them devastated by the loss. But it had been Beck who'd bonded the tightest with her during those last few months of her life and had held her hand when she'd taken her last breath.

Naming his firstborn daughter after Whitney had been his way of honoring their sister. Now, the name no longer brought sorrow, but happiness and joy to their family.

"How's my favorite niece?" Drew asked.

Beck rolled his eyes. "She's your *only* niece, dumbass."

He shrugged. "Which makes her my favorite."

"God, she's a handful," Beck said, shaking his head. "I don't know why they call them the terrible twos when that stubborn, sassy behavior lasts right through the threes."

"Don't listen to him. She's a perfect little angel." Chloe beamed as she dropped her phone back into the small purse she was carrying. "And if she exhibits a bit of headstrong behavior, well, I wonder where she gets that from, hmm?" She side-eyed her husband.

Drew laughed. "I cannot wait until she's a teenager and that rebellion really kicks in. Remember all the wild things we did? Sneaking out at night, meeting up with girls at the park and—"

"I'm keeping her locked in her bedroom until she's twenty-five," Beck muttered.

Drew arched a brow at his brother. "You can try, but even Rapunzel found a way to escape her tower and have some fun."

Beck glared, but truthfully, Drew had seen his brother with Whitney, and the little girl had him solidly wrapped around her finger. She was adorable, precocious, and sweet…if not a little stubborn.

The sound of someone tapping a microphone three times had everyone's attention turning toward the stage, where Aurora stood at a podium. She made the announcement that the bachelor auction was about to begin, and for the men to take their positions in the line-up.

"That's your cue to head on up to the butcher's block…I mean stage," his wise-ass brother said.

"Ha-ha," Drew replied in a droll tone. "You're such a comedian."

Drew glanced over to where he'd last seen Tripp, and saw him heading their way. He waited for his brother, then the two of them walked together to the stage.

"Enjoy your conversation with Skye?" Drew asked on the way.

Tripp gave him a startled look, which he quickly replaced with a more neutral expression. "How do you know Skye?"

"I don't. Chloe told me who you were talking to." He eyed Tripp more intently, wondering what his brother was hiding since he was keeping his replies vague. "You seem to be juggling a lot of women lately."

One corner of his brother's mouth tipped upward in an annoying smirk. "Jealous?"

"Hardly." Drew wasn't interested in women, as in *plural*, just one in particular that he had no business wanting as badly as he did.

Based on their number in the lineup, they stepped

up to their designated places on the stage, which put Drew next to Derek Bettencourt. He exchanged pleasantries with the other man, who seemed just as unenthused about being up for grabs as Drew was.

While Aurora spoke to the mostly female audience, encouraging the women to bid generously for a worthy cause, Drew glanced at the ladies gathered around the stage. Most of them appeared eager to win a weekend with one of New York City's most eligible bachelors but his perusal screeched to a halt when he saw Georgia in the crowd.

She stood next to another woman with similar facial features—the same female who'd been sitting next to her during the Leadership in Law dinner at Roland Brooks' table. Her sister, he assumed, and the differences between them were undeniable.

Their individual fashion style and appearance couldn't be more opposite. Georgia's modest beaded dress was a direct contrast to her sister's bohemian flowing gown, the silver bracelets up her arm, and the glittering ring in her nose. She had a free-spirit, nonconformist kind of vibe about her, while Georgia was more the type to follow decorum and rules. The same impression she'd given him during their conversation as they danced at the banquet.

Her sister had an arm through Georgia's as if to anchor her to her side so she didn't bolt. A distinct possibility since Georgia shifted from foot to foot, obviously uncomfortable being here. And though she wouldn't meet Drew's gaze, her sister stared straight at him, a mischievous smile on her lips. She gave him a surreptitious finger wave while Georgia wasn't looking, and he wasn't sure what to make of the action.

The auction began, and the first three guys went for decent amounts. Then it was Derek's turn, and the bidding war for him was insane, as well as amusing to watch because the two women who kept upping the ante clearly had some kind of rivalry going on between them.

Next, the auctioneer announced Drew, providing the audience with a brief introduction that highlighted his occupation and professional attributes before asking the standard opening question. "Who will start the bidding at ten-thousand-dollars for a three-day weekend with Drew Daniels?"

He did his best to stand tall and not wince at the awkward feeling.

"I'll start! Ten-thousand-dollars," a woman said from the audience, her voice coming through loud and clear.

Drew's gaze glanced in her direction, shocked to realize the bid came from Georgia's sister, who gave him a saucy wink and a satisfied grin. And when another woman bid after her, Georgia's sibling upped the ante. From the determined look on her face and the increased spending, she was *very* determined to win him.

He glanced at Georgia, who appeared as shocked at her sister's actions as he was.

Oh, hell. How fucking awkward would it be to entertain Georgia's sister for an entire weekend, when *Georgia* was the only woman he wanted?

✧   ✧   ✧

"COME ON, GEORGIA, I want to get a spot close to the front of the stage before the bidding starts."

Before Georgia could protest, Courtney linked their arms and started pulling her toward where Aurora was standing at a podium, announcing the beginning of the auction.

Her sister's grip kept Georgia by her side, and Courtney didn't release her even once they'd found a place close to the stage.

Georgia shifted in her heels and kept her gaze averted from the men all lined up, because she didn't want to risk Drew catching her looking at him, even accidentally.

"I really need to check on other things," Georgia said, trying to subtly untangle their arms, but her sister wasn't letting her go.

She didn't understand why Courtney was so insistent that Georgia join her, and the last thing she wanted to do was watch another woman win Drew for a weekend. It had been difficult enough being in the same ballroom with him for the past few hours, extremely aware of his presence. She'd done her best not to run into him and be forced into an awkward conversation. He'd made his feelings for her clear, and she was not a glutton for punishment.

"Like what?" Courtney challenged, arching a brow. "All the important stuff is done for the evening."

That was true. The event was at a point where she could just relax and enjoy the rest of the night, but witnessing other women vying for Drew's attention was not her idea of fun. "I should go and check the silent auction."

Courtney rolled her eyes at the excuse. "They call it a silent auction for a reason. It's *silent*, and nobody needs to be there for it to happen." Her sister sighed, giving Georgia one of those big, doe-eyed looks. "Come on, Georgie, you'll be my good luck charm. Besides, you need a break. I've been watching you flit about all evening, schmoozing with guests, checking on the catering and making sure everything is running smoothly."

Georgia shrugged. "That's my job."

"I know it is, which I respect, but can't you spare your sister a half hour of your time tonight?" This time, Courtney pulled out the big guns and batted her lashes at Georgia.

"Fine," Georgia relented.

Courtney laughed. "Geez, you don't have to sound so happy about it."

The auctioneer stepped up to the podium after Aurora was finished talking, introduced the first bachelor, and started the bidding process. Courtney bounced lightly on her feet, as if she was excited about the opportunity to bid.

Confused, Georgia leaned closer to her sister,

whose gaze was riveted to the stage. "I didn't think any of these guys would be your type," she said.

Courtney flashed her an enthusiastic grin. "Oh, I definitely have my eye on one man in particular."

Georgia couldn't imagine which one had caught her sister's attention. By all outward appearances, the bachelors were respectable businessmen, wearing tailored tuxedos and sporting well-groomed hair. Granted, they were all good-looking but much too conventional for Courtney's taste.

Now, if there had been a guy up there with tattoos and a leather jacket, and who rode a motorcycle—well, that kind of bad boy would appeal to her sister.

The first three men were auctioned off, followed by Derek Bettencourt, who'd given the entire ballroom quite a show as two women battled to win him until one of them finally tapped out as the bid reached an astronomical amount.

Then came Drew's turn, and the auctioneer introduced and described his attributes to the crowd. Georgia wanted nothing more than to disappear and not watch some other woman win a weekend with the man she desired. Somehow, she managed not to ogle him, despite the strong temptation to look his way.

"Who will start the bidding at ten-thousand-dollars for a three-day weekend with Drew Daniels?" the auctioneer asked.

"I'll start! Ten-thousand-dollars," Courtney called out before any other woman could.

Georgia's jaw dropped, and she stared at her sister

in shock.

Ignoring her, Courtney's expression was full of purpose, and as a few other women tried to outbid her, Courtney made it clear that she was out to win Drew.

Confusion rippled through Georgia, and she finally glanced up at Drew, but *he* was watching Courtney, looking just as perplexed as Georgia felt. Her sister knew who Drew was and had seen them dancing together at the banquet. Courtney had even teased Georgia over texts the next day, and Georgia had insisted there was nothing going on between her and Drew—which Courtney hadn't seemed to believe.

But now she was bidding on Drew…was her sister attracted to him, too?

"Drew Daniels, sold to the pretty woman with the silver bracelets on her arm," the auctioneer called out, his loud voice jarring Georgia back to the present. He pointed his gavel at Courtney. "Thank you for your very generous donation. You can meet your bachelor over in the greeting area just outside the ballroom."

"That would be me," Courtney said in a giddy tone and started toward the direction the auctioneer indicated, tugging Georgia along.

Still stunned, it took Georgia a moment to regain her bearings and pull back from Courtney's hold. "Wait."

Her sister stopped, a little frown forming between her brows. "What's wrong?"

Everything. "I don't need to be with you while you

meet Drew."

"Yes, you do," her sister insisted, smiling wide as she grabbed Georgia's hand. "I need you to introduce us."

She really wanted to refuse, and she'd be lying if she didn't admit that she was envious of Courtney winning this date with Drew. Jealous, even. But she didn't want to come across as petty. She'd already told her sister there was nothing between herself and Drew.

Georgia had had no claim on the man, and he'd already made it clear he didn't want *her*. So how could she begrudge her sister this date?

"Okay," Georgia said and exhaled a deep breath. She'd introduce them, then beeline it back into the ballroom and give Courtney and Drew time alone to get acquainted. Or maybe she'd stop in the ladies' room and be sick. That was also an option.

She followed Courtney to the greeting area, where the first four couples were chatting. Drew stood off to the side, his hands pushed into the front pockets of his trousers, and for the first time that evening, she really looked at his gorgeous face, expecting him to be watching her sister. Instead, his intense green eyes were focused on her as they approached.

She chewed anxiously on her bottom lip and when his warm, seductive gaze dropped to her mouth, her heart beat a little faster in her chest. His eyes lingered long enough to affirm the mutual awareness and attraction between them was still there despite what had happened at the banquet. Confusion still swarmed in her belly, not helped at all by his heated stare.

Just as she and Courtney reached him, he finally shifted his gaze to her sister, an amicable smile in place.

"Drew, this is my sister, Courtney. Courtney, Drew Daniels." Georgia quickly made the introductions. "The last thing you need is a third wheel, so I'll let the two of you get acquainted."

She turned to go, but once again Courtney caught her hand, stopping her.

"Wait. There's something I need to tell you."

Georgia forced herself to face her sister only to find a naughty glimmer of satisfaction sparkling in Courtney's eyes. "Happy birthday, Georgie."

She blinked at her sister, not sure what was going on. "What are you talking about? My birthday isn't until next weekend."

"I know that," Courtney said, her tone exasperated at Georgia's confusion. "*He's* your *early* birthday present." She waved her hand at Drew with a flourish, causing the bangles on her arm to make a tinkling sound. "I won him for *you*."

"You did what?" Georgia's eyes widened in shock while her face heated with mortification.

"I know you're not deaf," an amused Courtney said.

Drew let out a chuckle and Georgia wanted to die. She couldn't bring herself to look at him and discover what he really thought about this debacle.

Instead, she gave her sister a firm look. "Umm, can I talk to you *alone* for a moment?"

"Sure." Courtney smiled at Drew. "Excuse us for a second. We'll be right back."

"I'll be right here," he replied.

Georgia snuck a glance, and the corner of his mouth was quirked up in a grin.

She pulled her sister along this time, rushing them away from Drew. When she was certain they were out of earshot, she spun on her sister. "What are you doing?" she hissed.

"Matchmaking?" Courtney said, frowning at Georgia. "Why are you so upset? I thought I'd gotten you the best birthday gift ever."

Courtney had, except for the little problem that said birthday present wasn't interested. "There's nothing between us to matchmake."

Her sister laughed. "Oh, Georgie, you are so wrong. I saw the two of you at the awards banquet and the hot way Drew looked at you while you were dancing. And again tonight, his gaze followed you all around the ballroom while you did your best to keep your distance. All I'm doing is giving you a gentle push to go for it."

"Gentle?" she practically screeched. There was nothing gentle about a public bid on a man as if she were desperate. "And what do you mean, go for it?" Courtney sighed dramatically. "Go for *Drew*. Spend a weekend with him. Embrace the bad girl I know you've got inside of you *somewhere* beneath that responsible, conservative personality that keeps you from being daring and fearless."

Unable to formulate a thought, Georgia gaped at her sister, who wasn't finished. "Go have fun without overthinking things like you always do. Relax and enjoy yourself, and for God's sake, jump his bones, *multiple times* because he's fucking hot and you deserve some really good orgasms."

Georgia's entire body flashed with a heat that shimmied its way between her thighs at the thought of being so bold and uninhibited with Drew. She already knew what it felt like to be pressed against him so intimately, and she'd fantasized plenty about what he'd look like naked…and what he'd feel like, pulsing deep inside her.

Georgia shook her head, unable to do it. "That's your thing, not mine."

Courtney sighed. "Maybe, for once, it should be your thing, too."

She gave Georgia's hand an encouraging squeeze, then walked away, leaving Georgia alone with a decision to make.

Chapter Five

As soon as Courtney disappeared into the ballroom and Georgia started back toward Drew, he could see the indecision written all over her pretty face. She looked confused and conflicted, and he was the cause.

He'd sent all those mixed signals the night of the banquet, leaving her to believe he had no interest in pursuing her. Instead of it being the right move, his rejection had clearly hurt her. She wouldn't look him in the eye or speak to him all evening. He'd created this awkward tension between them, and now he needed to smooth things over.

And her firecracker of a sister had given him the opportunity.

When she finally reached where he was standing, he grinned, which did nothing to ease the wariness in both her posture and her expression.

"Your sister's quite feisty," he said, starting with a neutral topic.

She lifted her gaze to his, no warmth in her blue eyes, her walls high. "That's one word for her," she murmured.

He shoved his hands deeper into his pants pockets so he didn't reach out and skim his thumb along that faint scar on her chin, or worse, thread his fingers through her soft, silky-looking hair. "I think determined would be another good word."

She nodded in agreement and shifted anxiously in her heels while glancing around, anywhere but directly at him. He was aware of the other couples nearby, along with the auction echoing out to the meeting area and he didn't want to have this conversation with other people or distractions around. Preferring to be alone with her, he looked for somewhere quieter and more private.

Across the room were french doors that lead to an outdoor terrace. "I could use some fresh air," he said, angling his head in that direction. "How about you?"

She gave him a tight smile. "Sure."

They walked toward the exit, and Drew automatically placed his hand on the small of her back. She didn't step away or protest his touch, which he took as a good sign that maybe she was relaxing a bit—until they were alone on the terrace. When she turned to face him, she crossed her arms defensively over her chest.

Regardless of her attempt to remain guarded, the awareness was still strong between them, like an undeniable magnetic pull. He could see the desire in her moonlit eyes, in the softening of her features, and the slight parting of her lips as their gazes met and held. And despite every reason not to, Drew selfishly wanted to explore the connection they'd shared the night they met—before he'd royally screwed things up.

Right or wrong, this woman made him feel things that went beyond mere attraction, and he just knew he'd regret letting her go a second time.

"I'm really sorry about this…situation," Georgia said, her words coming out in a rush. "I had no idea that Courtney intended to bid on you. I mean, I know that you're not interested in me that way—"

"Here's the problem, Georgia," he said, cutting off her nervous rambling and taking a step closer to her. "I'm *very* interested in you."

She scoffed in disbelief. "You don't need to flatter me. I got the message loud and clear the night of the banquet."

Oh, yeah, he'd hurt her, and he felt like a jerk for doing so. "I don't think you got the *right* message," he said, ready to flip this script in a more convincing manner. "The one I should have been conveying."

A small frown creased her brows, her ongoing confusion obvious. She'd had too many ups and downs tonight, and it was time he set things straight.

He placed his hands against the sides of her neck and used his thumbs to tip her head back a bit to make sure he had her full attention.

She swallowed hard, her eyes fixed on his. "What message?"

"This one," he said, and dropped his mouth to hers.

Her lips parted on a shocked gasp, and he didn't

hesitate to deepen the kiss while he had the chance, his tongue sweeping inside to find and tangle with hers. Her hands came up to his chest, and for a moment he thought for sure she was going to shove him away, but her fingers curled into the fabric of his dress shirt, and the sweetest, hottest moan escaped her throat as the tension in her body finally dissipated.

Lust surged through his veins as he continued to kiss her hungrily, and he reveled in her unbridled response as their mouths consumed each other. He was immediately addicted to her taste, and he wanted more. She swayed toward him, equally greedy, in a way that hinted at a very sensual creature lurking beneath the surface of her demure, composed personality.

His cock hardened as he thought of all things he'd love to do to her, just to hear her beg as he sucked her nipples, or watch her unravel as he used his mouth, tongue, and fingers between her thighs until she was shaking and wrung out from multiple orgasms before burying himself to the hilt inside her soft, warm body.

He wanted all that with Georgia, and so much more.

He had to force himself to slow things down, and when he finally lifted his lips from hers, she made a soft sound of protest that made him grin.

Still holding her face in his hands, her lashes fluttered open, and she looked up at him, all the earlier misgivings he'd seen etched across her expression now gone. Her cheeks were flushed, her lips swollen from his kisses, and her eyes glimmered with pleasure.

In that moment, he knew he wouldn't pass up the opportunity to spend a weekend with her. He told himself the purpose would be to attempt to dilute this intense attraction between them but even he knew deep down, he was lying. He'd never get enough.

She exhaled a delicate breath, the corner of her mouth curving up in a soft smile. "That was, um, some message."

He chuckled and pressed his forehead to hers. "I was an idiot that night. I thought I was doing the right thing by walking away, but the truth is, I haven't been able to get you out of my head."

She tipped her head slightly. "What do you mean by 'the right thing'?"

Releasing a deep breath, he stroked his thumb along her jaw. The situation with Elliott was complicated and Drew had no desire to talk about the other man and all the bad history between them. Not when the time he had with Georgia was undoubtedly limited. He'd yet to make a firm decision about taking on the European client, but he was leaning in that direction. How could he not? But once he accepted his boss's offer, he'd have very little time to spend with Georgia.

"It doesn't matter," he said. "But *you* do. If next weekend is your birthday, then let's go somewhere, celebrate and have fun, just the two of us. We could get to know one another better under more casual circumstances. Share a few more of those hot kisses…and maybe *other things*."

Yeah, he was being presumptuous, but the flash of

desire in her eyes told him that they were on the same page.

"I'd like that," she said breathlessly.

Relief and elation surged through him. "I just need to clear my calendar and check in with my boss. Make sure my assistant is up to speed on my open cases, should something come up."

She bit her bottom lip—not anxiously this time, but seductively. "So, where should we go?"

He thought of all the possibilities, but already knew where he wanted to take her—somewhere personal and special. Most women he knew or dated would expect a lavish, extravagant time—and he could certainly afford to give Georgia the same—but he had a feeling she'd appreciate a more thoughtful and sincere choice instead.

"Why don't you leave that up to me as a surprise?" he said.

Excitement lit her eyes. "Okay," she whispered, and he couldn't resist kissing her again. This time slower and softer and more seductive.

He couldn't wait to get her alone and all to himself.

Chapter Six

THE FOLLOWING FRIDAY, Georgia left work early to head home and pack for her birthday weekend with Drew, unable to contain her excitement for whatever lay ahead.

It had seemed like the longest week ever—her thoughts consumed with Drew, the seductive kiss they'd shared at the charity event that proved their mutual attraction was real, and the random texts he'd sent her over the past few days that ranged from sweet, to amusing, to flirtatious. Whatever had held him back from pursuing her at the Leadership in Law banquet was gone.

She'd been floating on a high, smiling so much that Billie and Aurora had commented on her perma-grin and the reason for it since they both knew the story about Courtney's unconventional birthday gift.

She arrived at her apartment, and just as she retrieved her small suitcase and set it on her bed to pack, a brisk knock sounded at her door. She checked the peephole, and seeing her sister standing on the other side, she let Courtney in.

"What are you doing here?" Georgia asked in surprise.

Her sister held out a flat, rectangular box that was wrapped in festive birthday paper with a bow on top. "I wanted to drop this off before you left since I won't be seeing you for your birthday tomorrow."

Georgia accepted the gift with a frown. "You already bought me a birthday present, and an expensive one at that. You didn't need to get me anything else."

"Sure I did." Courtney grinned. "It's just a little something I thought you might enjoy."

Georgia was definitely curious to know what was inside. "Can I open it?"

"Not until you arrive wherever you're going," her sister said with a shake of her head. "Speaking of which, where is Drew taking you?"

Georgia walked back to her bedroom to finish packing while she chatted with her sister. "I honestly don't know," she said, putting the gift into her suitcase to open later. "He didn't give me any details. Just said it would be a surprise and to pack casually."

Courtney made herself comfortable sitting up against the pillows on Georgia's bed. "Oooh, I love a man with initiative." She waggled her brows. "Are you excited?"

Georgia's answer came easily. "Yes, I am."

She was looking forward to getting to know Drew better, to see if their chemistry was more than just physical. There was no denying he fascinated her, and in a short time made her feel things no one else ever had. There was so much to like about him, and this weekend would hopefully lead to something deeper for them both.

"So, what did you tell Mom and Dad about where you're going?" Courtney asked, knowing that their parents—their mother, especially—always liked to celebrate their birthdays out at dinner somewhere as a family.

"I told Mom that I was spending the weekend away with a friend," she said, since Courtney had kept winning Drew for her birthday a secret between them. "Of course Mom wasn't happy because she'd invited Elliott to join us for dinner, and now she had to cancel and disappoint him."

Courtney stuck her finger in her mouth and made a gagging sound, and Georgia laughed as she placed a folded stack of clothes into her luggage, then added a couple of pairs of shoes.

While Georgia finished packing, they chatted a bit more, discussing the abstract and sometimes whimsical sculptures Courtney created, and the gallery interested in taking them on consignment. When Drew sent Georgia a text letting her know he was on his way to pick her up, Courtney decided it was time for her to leave.

Georgia walked her sister to the door and gave her a hug. "Thank you again for my birthday gift," she said.

Courtney tossed her hair back and grinned. "Enjoy your time with that hot, sexy man. And don't do anything that I wouldn't do."

Georgia rolled her eyes. "Well, that leaves the field wide open now, doesn't it?"

"That's the point," her sister said, winking at Georgia.

Once Courtney was gone, Georgia finished packing her toiletries and her sexiest lingerie and underwear, which wasn't saying much since she'd bought the pieces more for comfort and practicality than seduction, she thought with a grimace. She should have thought ahead and picked up some things, but at least everything was fairly new, and there were bits of lace here and there.

She changed into a pair of dark denim jeans, a long-sleeved loose blouse in a shade of light blue, and a pair of flats. Just as she zipped up her suitcase and rolled it to the front room, another knock sounded at the door.

Unable to suppress the giddy sensation fluttering in her stomach, she opened the door, feasting her eyes on the man who'd been in the forefront of her thoughts all week. She'd only seen him wearing suits, but he was equally gorgeous in a green Henley with the sleeves pushed up to reveal his strong, sexy forearms, and a pair of form-fitting jeans. His dark hair was a bit ruffled, and his green eyes went dark as soon as he saw her.

Without any verbal greeting, he stepped toward Georgia, threaded his fingers in her hair, tipped her head back, and pressed his mouth to hers. The unexpected kiss was slow and soft at first—a sweet, tentative hello that made her melt against him like warm taffy. But as soon as she moaned in acquiescence and parted her lips, he didn't hesitate to slide his tongue against hers, tasting her, ravishing her.

Pure sensation shot through every part of her body—her breasts, her belly, and a low ache between her thighs throbbed and ached. She wasn't sure what to do with her hands, so she settled them on his hips as sparks erupted between them, making her crave this kiss, his strength, and the hard length of his cock she felt pressed against her. She loved everything about the way he claimed her…from the silkiness of his tongue, the warmth of his breath, and the flavor of mint lingering on his lips.

With a low, rumbling growl in his throat, he gradually lifted his mouth from hers, then stared down at her face with unmistakable hunger gleaming in the depths of his eyes. She shivered as he skimmed his thumb down her cheek and then along her damp bottom lip, tugging gently.

"I've been waiting all week to kiss you again," he said huskily.

His words thrilled her. Emboldened her. "You can kiss me anytime."

He groaned. "You're making it very difficult for me to restrain myself," he warned.

This weekend, she didn't want him to hold back. She wasn't brave enough to voice those thoughts just yet, but she was definitely going to take her sister's words to heart and enjoy her weekend, and whatever it entailed, with Drew.

Very reluctantly, he released her. "Ready to head out?"

She nodded. "I am."

She grabbed her purse, he picked up her suitcase, and together they walked to his car—a silver, sporty Audi. He put her luggage in the trunk next to his own, then opened the passenger door for her—which she appreciated—before sliding into the driver's seat.

He started up the vehicle and glanced at her. "It's about a two-and-a-half-hour drive to where we're going," he said, still keeping their destination a secret. "I thought we could stop at a pizza joint I know on the way for dinner. Does that sound okay to you?"

She nodded, her stomach rumbling at the suggestion. "Sounds perfect."

They headed out of the city, their conversation light and easy and mainly revolving around what their week at work entailed. An hour and a half later, he turned into a parking lot and stopped his car near a brick building. It was dusk by now, but she could see that the place, Otto's Pizzeria, was well-maintained and fairly busy on a Friday evening.

The inside décor was old school with rich wooden tables and chairs, red and white checkered tablecloths, and soft lighting. Signs boasted authentic Sicilian pizza, and she loved that he didn't pick anything fancy or expensive to try and impress her. He was a man who was confident in his choices, no matter what they were, and that in itself was sexy and remarkable.

Surprisingly, they were able to secure a table fairly quickly, and after agreeing on a sausage and mushroom combination, and their two sodas were delivered, they were left alone.

Georgia realized that while she'd divulged quite a bit about herself when she'd danced with him at the banquet—her job with Future Fast Track, and even giving him a glimpse of her family dynamic—he'd been vague about himself. Most of their conversations about him had been superficial, and she was curious to know what shaped Drew into the man he was today.

Glancing across the table at him, she braced her elbows on the surface and laced her fingers beneath her chin. "So, you know all about me and my non-profit work. What made you want to practice law?"

A sexy grin tipped up the corner of his mouth. "Growing up, I watched a lot of old episodes of *Boston Legal*, *Suits*, and *Law and Order* with my dad, and I was always fascinated by the courtroom scenes and deliberations. I was also captain on the debate team in high school, and we won the state championship in my junior and senior years. Being a lawyer just seemed like a natural fit."

She arched her brow and took a drink of her soda. "So, you like to argue and win."

He chuckled, his green eyes gleaming with amusement. "I think my brothers would agree with that statement."

"And out of all the areas of law you could choose from, you went into mergers and acquisitions. Interesting choice."

"Looks like someone has been doing her home-work," he drawled, clearly impressed with her knowledge.

"I'll admit, I Googled you," she said with a shrug, then rattled off a few more details she'd learned. "You work at McKenzie Goodwin, which is a competitor to my father's firm, as you probably already know."

He nodded, but said nothing, so she continued.

"And quite impressively, you made partner a year ago and you're only thirty-four," she said, smiling. She'd read about the huge, lucrative deal that had most likely contributed to that promotion. "That's quite an achievement."

"It is," he agreed, but didn't brag about that major accomplishment, as most men might.

Unlike Elliott, this man had nothing to prove to anyone but himself. He was confident without being arrogant. Assertive in his work life—a requirement for most attorneys—but without an overblown ego. Drew was completely unpretentious despite his successes, and it was those traits that she found so attractive and appealing.

Their pizza was delivered, and after they'd enjoyed a slice and went for seconds, Georgia contemplated why Elliott was so hostile toward Drew when she couldn't find any outward indications that the man sitting across from her was untrustworthy, as Elliott had suggested the night of the banquet. They both practiced the same type of law, but that still didn't explain Elliott's animosity.

"What's going on between you and Elliott?" she asked as they finished their meal and the bill was delivered. She hoped Drew might shed some light on things.

Drew took out his wallet and pulled out a few large bills—more than enough to cover the tab and tip—and set the cash on the table. "What makes you think there's something going on?"

His expression gave nothing away, but she'd seen and felt the underlying strain during the banquet. "There just seems to be an odd tension between you two."

Drew hesitated for a moment before replying in an even tone, "I have nothing against Elliott, and do you really want to talk about him this weekend?"

It was a fair question, and made her realize that a conversation about Elliott had the potential to lead to her own issues with the man, along with her parent's hopes and expectations, and that was the last thing she wanted to discuss.

"No, I don't," she said.

Relief chased across Drew's features, and he seemed to relax. "Good, because he's the last person I want interfering with my weekend with you."

Okay, put that way, Georgia completely understood and agreed, because the only thing she wanted to concentrate and focus on the next few days was *this* man.

Drew stood up and held his hand out to her.

"Ready to get out of here?"

She nodded, and without thinking, she placed her hand in his, as if it were the most natural thing in the world to do. "Let's do this."

BY THE TIME they reached the Catskill Mountain region half an hour later, it was completely dark out. Drew turned off onto a familiar private drive, catching a glimpse of the small frown on Georgia's face as she tried to see something in the pitch-blackness around them beyond the beams of his car's headlights and the large trees on either side of the road.

The road was secluded and remote, as was the place they were headed, and for a moment, Drew experienced a stab of uncertainty about the plans he'd made. What if he'd judged wrong, and she expected something more extravagant and lavish? He supposed if she really hated this idea, he could always take her to one of the luxury, all-inclusive resorts located nearby.

"Where are we?" she asked, still straining to see what was ahead. "You're either taking me camping out in the wild, or you're a serial killer and this is the perfect deserted place to hide my body."

He chuckled. "Neither, and you're clearly watching too many murder mysteries."

She gave him an adorably impish look. "You're probably right. Those shows are my guilty pleasure."

"Mine, too," he admitted, surprised to discover his

sweet Georgia had a devious side. "It's always the spouse, am I right?"

She grinned. "Nine times out of ten, and there's usually a hefty insurance policy involved."

He drove around a curve in the road, and a single structure in the distance came into view. The porch light was on, as were a few of them inside the place, so they weren't walking into pitch darkness.

Georgia sat up in her seat as he finally parked the car in front of the small house. "What is this place?" she asked curiously.

He glanced at her, trying to gauge her reaction. "It's my family's cabin...and if you aren't comfortable staying here, we can get a room at a nearby resort."

"Are you kidding me?" she said, her voice infused with excitement. "I love this idea. The highlight of my summers growing up was sleepaway camp. Just tell me there's a working toilet and I don't have to worry about using an outhouse."

He chuckled in relief. "Water, plumbing, heating, and electricity are all in working order. It might look a little rustic on the outside, but all the important amenities are included, I promise."

Even in the dim interior of his vehicle, he could see the happy sparkle in her eyes. "Okay, then I'm good."

They got out of the car and met up at the trunk, and while he retrieved both of their suitcases, she stared up at the structure, taking it all in. The exterior had been built to look like a classic log cabin, with a wide front porch. During the day, there was a spectac-ular view of the forest and mountain range, and at night, like now, the sky was clear and filled with an abundance of bright stars.

The property was three acres of privacy and na-ture, yet civilization and the nearest town was only a fifteen minute drive away.

"Why are the lights on inside?" she asked as they headed up the porch stairs. "Is someone already here?"

"No. We're alone for the weekend." He set one of the bags down to open the door with the key his mother had given him this past week. "It's been a while since me or any family members have been here, so I had property management come and clean the place and stock the kitchen with the food and items I requested for the weekend."

As they entered, the inside smelled fresh and clean, and as always, he was hit with so many fun and fond memories of spending time here. While Georgia took in the open floor plan that included a decent sized living room, an updated kitchen, and a dining table, he set their luggage down and gave her a quick rundown of the history of the place.

"My parents purchased the cabin when me and my siblings were young kids, and we came up here at least three times a year. Spring, summer, and fall," he told her…up until his sister had been diagnosed with cancer, and everything had changed in their family. Once Whitney passed away, it hadn't been the same, and then he and his brothers had all gone off to college, one by one.

"My parents still come up here occasionally," he said after clearing the gruff emotions from his throat. "But now that my brothers and I are all grown, the place really is too small for all of us to be here at the same time, though I do come up here on occasion. Like when I just need to relax and decompress."

"I can see why." She ran her fingers along the books lined up on a shelf near the fireplace—thrillers and mysteries and spy novels for his father, and the romance books his mother enjoyed. "The place is very cozy."

"Let me show you around," he said, taking her hand and guiding her toward the back of the cabin. "It's small and only two bedrooms, so the tour shouldn't take long," he added with a grin.

They came to the main bedroom first, complete with a king-sized bed and adjoining bathroom, then he pointed out the single bathroom that he and his siblings had to share and fight over. He switched on the light to the second bedroom, revealing the same double twin bunk beds that had been there since his youth, which had accommodated him, his brothers, and Whitney.

"My parents really should convert this into a guest room," he said in a wry tone. "But my mother insists that she needs beds for her grandkids to stay here someday."

Georgia laughed and stepped inside, taking in the

quilts on the bed and then gravitating toward the framed photos on the dresser. "She sounds hopeful."

He braced his shoulder against the door frame, watching her examine the snapshots of him and his siblings in this mountain element. "Well, Beck is at least fulfilling that dream of hers."

She glanced at him with a teasing grin. "Aren't you going to contribute to the cause?"

"Not anytime soon," he replied, hating that little punch in the gut that felt a whole lot like regret, but knew he had to keep his reply honest. "Being partner keeps me insanely busy with little time to give to a relationship, let alone get married and have a family that I can't be there for."

She nodded, as if understanding, but he didn't miss the disappointment in her eyes as she returned to the pictures. He felt like a jerk for being so blunt, but as much as he wanted Georgia, he'd learned a valuable lesson with Angie, that it wasn't fair to any woman to make promises he wasn't sure he could keep at this point in his life, when his career was literally in the fast lane. The last thing he wanted to do was lead Georgia to believe he was capable of or ready for a long-term commitment.

Georgia picked up a framed picture of him and his siblings standing next to their father, all of them with cheesy grins on their faces as they each held up their own trout they'd caught. His mother had taken the photo right before Tripp had shoved Beck into the river behind them, taunting their youngest brother that he was going to feed *him* to the fish, which had totally freaked Beck out and made him scream like a girl and run out of the water.

Fun times. The memory made him smile.

"You have a sister?" Georgia asked of the young girl in the photo. She glanced his way and tipped her head curiously as she set the frame back down.

"Had a sister, yes," he corrected her. "That's Whitney, Tripp's twin. She died of leukemia at the age of sixteen."

Georgia gasped in shock. "I'm so sorry," she said softly, her eyes filled with genuine sympathy. "That must have been incredibly difficult for your entire family."

"It was. We miss her a lot," he said, realizing Georgia was one of the few women in his life that knew that part of his past now, information he'd *wanted* to share with her.

His sister's passing wasn't a topic of conversation he had with the random females he hooked up with, but Georgia was already starting to feel like more than just a casual weekend fling, despite knowing that's all it really could be with her.

Wanting a distraction from those troubling thoughts, he pushed away from the doorframe and angled his head toward the back of the cabin. "Come on. There's something else I want to show you."

She followed him out a back door, which led to a large deck with a wood burning firepit table, and cushioned chairs and lounge seats that had been cleaned and set out for the weekend. Beneath an enclosed cedar gazebo was a hot tub that was currently covered. He turned on a switch, and the string of lights overhead lit up, giving the enclosure a more romantic ambiance.

"I had the management company clean out the hot tub and fill it with fresh water. Since it's still fairly early, care to relax and unwind in the hot tub with a glass of wine?"

She nodded enthusiastically. "That sounds amazing. I brought a swimsuit like you suggested."

"Bummer." He gave her a wicked grin as he removed the cover on the spa and then fired up the jets to get the water heating. "I was hoping you'd forgotten, and we could skinny dip."

Even with just the string of lights overhead, he could see the blush rise on her cheeks. "Umm, yeah...I think I need to work up to that."

He chuckled. "Fair enough."

He watched her head back inside the cabin while he made sure everything was in working order with the hot tub, well aware that seeing Georgia in a clinging bathing suit was going to be just as torturous—as well as a testament to just how strong his restraint truly was.

Chapter Seven

GEORGIA'S SUITCASE WAS still in the living room where Drew had left it when they'd walked into the cabin, and since she was unsure where he planned for her to sleep, she waited for him to finish setting up the hot tub outside and join her. Which gave her way too much time to think about her heartbreaking conversation with him about his sister…and the subtle warning he'd given her about not having the time to give to a committed relationship.

At least, that's how his comment had come across, as a way of cautioning her not to read into this weekend with him as anything more than a birthday gift.

Good to know where things stood, she thought, staring out the front window of the cabin to the darkness beyond. She appreciated his honesty, even if she did feel a twinge of disappointment. But at least she now knew to temper her expectations and just enjoy her time with Drew for what it was. A sexy, fun weekend fling.

Definitely sexy. Drew had certainly given off those seductive vibes when he'd suggested they skinny dip, and a part of her was tempted to throw caution to the wind and do just that…

"Is everything okay?"

Georgia jumped at the sound of Drew's deep voice behind her, her heart jolting in her chest. She'd been so immersed in her thoughts that she hadn't heard him come back inside. She turned around, gathered her composure, and nodded.

"I wasn't sure which room you wanted me to use," she said. "Where would you like me to sleep?"

Something hot and sinful smoldered in his green eyes, and she could easily guess the answers filling his mind…*in his bed…beneath him…with his cock nestled between her thighs.* Or maybe those were her own fantasies playing out in her head.

Finally, he said, "You can have the main bedroom. I'll take one of the bunk beds."

She suddenly realized how ridiculous and uncomfortable that would be, his tall, broad frame unable to truly fit on a short, narrow, twin-size mattress. She shook her head. "You know what, I'll take one of the bunk beds."

"Not negotiable," he said, smiling as he picked up her luggage and headed toward the larger room, forcing her to follow. "It's your birthday, and I insist."

"Okay."

"I'll be back in a few minutes," he said after placing her suitcase on the bed. "I'm going to go change into my swim shorts."

Once he was gone, she unzipped her bag and dug through the contents to search for her swimsuit. She found the two separate pieces just as she came across the gift that Courtney had given her earlier that day. She pulled out the wrapped box, and with curiosity getting the best of her, she set her bikini aside and ripped off the paper and opened the present.

A small note card sat on top of the folded pink tissue, which read, *Don't waste this chance to go for it...*

Such simple words, but with so much meaning coming from her sister. Tentatively, she pulled back the tissue paper and felt her face heat and her stomach flip as she took in the assortment of erotic items: a silk blindfold mask, fur-lined handcuffs, and a feather tickler. In addition to those toys was something red, sheer, and lacy, and she lifted up the lingerie to see a provocative babydoll nightie and matching panties, whose sole purpose was to tease and entice.

"That's quite a present."

Startled once again by Drew's deep, husky drawl, Georgia immediately dropped the nightie back into the box, certain he'd seen all the other goodies inside since he was now standing close by. Mortification rushed through her.

"Yeah, my sister is such a jokester," she said, putting the lid back on top and stuffing the box back into her luggage, doing her best to avoid eye contact with Drew. "I think I could use that glass of wine right about now."

He chuckled, the sound filled with amusement. "Put on your swimsuit and meet me at the hot tub," he said, and to her immense relief he walked back out of the room without saying anything more, *thank God.*

She clipped her hair on top of her head to keep it from getting wet and quickly changed into her bikini, a rather modest two-piece that kept her full breasts decently concealed, and high-waisted bottoms that covered her ass and the part of her stomach she liked the least. But it didn't matter how demure her choice of swimwear was, because as soon as she walked out back and Drew turned to look at her, she felt bare and exposed.

He stood by the side of the tub, two glasses of wine sitting on the rim along with the half empty bottle, and he didn't bother to hide his desire as his hooded gaze raked down the length of her like a heated caress. She shivered—and not from the cool night air brushing over her skin—and her nipples tightened into hard peaks against the thin fabric of her bikini top.

He noticed, his eyes lingering on her breasts before finally lifting to her face. He ran his tongue along his bottom lip as if he were hungry to taste her, and she fervently wished that mouth of his was sliding across her bare skin. He made her feel sexy and desirable, and confident, and she embraced the sensations.

And because turnabout's fair play and she was feeling a little daring herself, she let her own eyes take in his half naked body—from his broad shoulders down to his muscular chest, then along his firm, toned abs to the waistband of his swim trunks sitting low on his lean hips. He was in great shape, and when her gaze dropped a little lower and she saw the impressive outline of his cock against the front of his swim shorts, she bit her bottom lip.

"Stop staring at me like that," he growled, the dark, dangerous tone of his voice making her shiver.

She brought her eyes back up to his and smiled flirtatiously. "*You* started it."

He narrowed his gaze, trying to appear stern, but the playful smile tugging on his lips gave him away. "Even if I did, you're tempting me to say fuck being a gentleman and instead trace your gorgeous curves with my hands, followed by my mouth, then my tongue. Preferably while you're naked."

Her breath caught, and before she could stop herself, the truth spilled out of her in a sassy retort. "Maybe I want you to."

Both of his brows rose as she strolled over to where he was standing by the stairs leading up to the hot tub. Just as she started up the first one, he smacked her on the ass with his hand, just enough to sting and make her gasp in shock.

She stopped and stared at him with wide eyes, though she hadn't found the swat unpleasant at all, but rather…arousing. "What was *that* for?"

He burned her with a hot, possessive look. "Don't make promises you don't intend to keep."

"Duly noted," she whispered, even knowing she was going to take her sister's advice and *go for it* with this man. She had nothing to lose and everything to gain in terms of pleasure and the kind of heady passion she'd yet to experience.

They settled into the hot tub next to each other with glasses of wine while Drew regaled her with amusing childhood stories about the pranks he and his siblings pulled on one another and their fun times at the cabin, most of which made her laugh. Other than losing his sister as a teenager, his upbringing seemed so normal and carefree, which she envied.

It also made her realize she didn't have these kinds of lighthearted stories to share in return. Which made her incredibly sad.

"I wish I had that kind of carefree youth," she said softly, the glass of wine having not only relaxed her body, but her mind, too. "Being the oldest, I was always expected to be on my best behavior at all times, conforming to my parents' rules and trying to fulfill their expectations of what they wanted me to be. That whole oldest child syndrome."

"And your sister?" he asked, setting his empty wineglass at the corner of the tub, along with hers, while bubbles and steam rose from the heated, churning water around them. "Were the same things expected of her?"

Georgia sighed as the tub jets massaged her lower back. "Courtney was the wild child, still is actually. She was always stubborn, too, and my mother could never tame my sister's bigger-than-life personality, and eventually, she gave up trying, which put even more pressure on me to behave." Realizing how resentful that might sound, she quickly added, "Don't get me wrong. I adore my sister and how easygoing she is and how she just doesn't care what other people think about her. Honestly, I wish I were more like her."

Drew stretched his arms along the rim of the tub, his fingers lazily trailing along her wet shoulder and up to the side of her neck. "In what way?"

"Not giving a damn what people think and pursuing what makes me happy instead of always trying to be a people pleaser," she said, finding it much too easy to open up to Drew—maybe because he didn't judge her for her honest feelings. "Being bold and daring and not thinking about the consequences."

"You can still be that person," he said, his tone wry. "In fact, I think you're more rebellious than you give yourself credit for. You took a job that you enjoyed, not what your parents expected, and then there's that tiny scar on your chin, and the fact that you refused to have it removed with cosmetic surgery, which speaks for itself."

It surprised her that he remembered so much of what she'd told him that first night they'd met at the banquet. "Yes, I suppose so."

A sinfully seductive smile lifted the corner of his mouth as the tips of his fingers feathered along her jaw. "But if you're looking to be bad in other ways, I'm more than happy to help with that." He winked at her.

This was it, Georgia realized. He'd just issued a very enticing invitation and was waiting for her to accept or decline. He was giving her all the power without pressure…and there was only one choice she wanted to make. She didn't want to leave this weekend having any regrets.

She scooted across the seat toward him, then let the water carry her over his lap so that she could straddle him where he sat. She clutched her knees against his hips and placed her hands on his shoulders, unable to believe just how brazen she was being.

He looked up at her, his satisfied grin slow but wolfish, while his hands gradually slid down her back. Beneath the water, he grabbed her ass and hauled her closer, spreading her thighs wider and deliberately pressing the hard length of his erection right between her legs. Heat and excitement spiraled through her, making her core clench and pulse with the need to grind against that solid, significant bulge.

His eyes shone with a teasing, taunting light. "Show me what a bad, dirty girl you can be, Georgia," he said huskily.

Completely emboldened by his words, she framed his face in her hands, feeling the abrasion of his slight stubble against her palms as she settled her mouth against his and kissed him. Every other time he'd been in control, but tonight, he let her take the reins, and she didn't hesitate to deepen the connection, chasing his tongue with her own and reveling in the low, unraveling groan that rumbled in his chest.

Waves of heat rolled through her, and there was no thinking of anything else but this man and the way her body responded to him, the way he made her *feel*.

Wild, free, and completely liberated, she began gyrating her hips, rubbing her aching sex against that rigid column of flesh, fervently wishing they were naked. She desperately needed direct stimulation and friction against her clit, and she moaned in frustration against his lips.

She broke their kiss and tipped her head back, guiding his mouth to her neck as she continued to rock against him, seeking relief from the building pressure. His lips seared her skin, and his hot, damp tongue traveled down to the hollow of her throat. She arched her back, lifting her breasts higher, and with her hands twisting in his hair she pulled his head down.

She might not be able to make herself say the words, *suck my breasts*, but he was a smart man and knew what she wanted. His mouth opened around a stiff nipple, pulling and biting on the bead of flesh through the fabric of her bikini top, and she cried out, panting, so close to the release just out of her reach…

"Goddamn," Drew rasped, grabbing on to her hips to stop the rolling, thrusting movements she was making against his cock.

She made a distinct sound of displeasure and frowned down at him. "Why did you stop?"

"It wasn't easy. Trust me," he said, breathing hard as a muscle in his jaw twitched. "But if I'm going to make you come, it's not going to be in a hot tub. Not the first time. I want you spread out naked on a bed, so I can bury my face between your thighs and fuck you with my tongue and feel you come all over my fingers. And then, I want to make you come again, this time around my cock."

She whimpered at the provocative images he'd put in her head. "I would like that very much, please."

He groaned out a laugh at her too prim and proper reply. "You're so fucking sweet. You're killing me, Georgia. You know that?"

"No, I want to *please* you," she said, leaning back toward him and brushing her lips across his, prepared to shed every last bit of her modesty in the pursuit of pleasure. "Whatever you want, however you want it."

He swore under his breath. "Go get in the shower while I turn off the jets and cover the tub. I want all the chlorine washed off so I can lick your skin and taste *you.*"

She shuddered with need and rushed to do as he instructed.

DREW DIDN'T WASTE any time outside, quickly shutting off the hot tub and taking their empty glasses and wine bottle to the kitchen. The last thing he wanted to do was give Georgia too much time to change her mind, not when she'd issued him such an enticing invitation. Her provocative words, *whatever you want, however you want it,* had his cock hard as stone and his mind racing with all the possibilities.

This woman tempted him beyond all reason and

not just physically, as was evidenced by his already rock-hard dick. There was just something so real and genuine about Georgia. There were no pretenses with her, as he was used to with other women, and she was so uncertain of her own sensuality. She was clearly used to being the good girl, which was why he'd challenged her to be a bad girl with him.

It was all the prompting she'd needed to do something reckless and impulsive. The fact that she'd straddled his lap out in the hot tub and gave him the equivalent of an erotic lap dance that had given him an immediate boner, but she'd also given him a glimpse of her naughtier side. Which he liked...a lot.

If he had his way, by the end of their weekend together he will have fucked every last bit of her inhibitions out of her. The thought pleased him, until a small voice in his head reminded him that another man would eventually reap those benefits, and not him. Which made him feel possessive as hell, even though he knew he had no business feeling anything for her that would complicate this weekend arrangement.

By the time he reached the main bathroom, Georgia was just stepping beneath the warm shower spray to rinse off, still wearing her bikini.

"Why are you still in your swimsuit?" he asked, frowning at her.

Her cheeks flushed, as if she were hesitant to be the first one to strip naked. "Why are you?" she shot back cheekily.

He smirked and didn't hesitate to shuck his wet swim trunks, releasing his stiff, aching cock to her gaze. She sucked in a startled breath, her pretty blue eyes wide and shocked as she stared at his full-blown erection.

"Your turn," he ordered gruffly. "Take off your top."

Biting her bottom lip, she untied the strings holding up her bikini top and let the material covering her lush breasts fall to the floor. He groaned at the sight of those gorgeous, bare tits he couldn't wait to get his hands and mouth on, and joined her in the shower stall. The enclosure hadn't exactly been built to accommodate two people, which made the space more intimate since neither of them could move without their bodies brushing the other's.

He filled his palms with the fragrant liquid soap, and beginning at her shoulders, he started washing her skin…sliding his hands along her arms, then across her chest, and down to her breasts. He plucked at her nipples as he leaned in and kissed her slow and deep, while pushing her back up against the shower wall and aligning his chest to hers.

Her slick, soapy skin rubbed against his, and he let his hands wander lower, mapping out her curves as the water cascaded over the both of them, until he reached the waistband of her bottoms. He pushed the material down her hips and over her ass, and the wet, clinging fabric slid down her legs to join the top piece on the shower floor.

He lifted his mouth from hers, staring down into her hazy eyes as he continued stroking his slippery palm along the inside of her thighs in a teasing caress. "So, in the spirit of full disclosure, I want you to know before we go any further that I did bring condoms, but I also recently had my yearly physical and I'm clean."

"Same," she said breathlessly when his thumb brushed the lips of her pussy, her hips rolling toward his hand for a deeper touch, which he didn't grant just yet. "And I'm on birth control."

He allowed a slow, seductive smile to tip up the corner of his mouth. "Then how I fuck you is completely up to you."

"I want you bare," she whispered without any hesitation.

His cock pulsed at the thought of being inside her with nothing between them. "Then let's get you rinsed off so I can fuck you properly on a nice, soft bed."

He removed the handheld showerhead from the holder and let the spray chase away the last of the soap on her skin. The water splashed against her breasts, and she moaned softly as he continued along her abdomen, and lower still. Maneuvering his foot between hers, he pushed her legs apart and aimed the stream directly at her exposed clit.

Her entire body jerked at the contact, and she grabbed on to his biceps, her lips parting as she started to pant. "Drew…" Her head fell against the wall, and her eyes rolled back as he moved the showerhead in a rhythmic circular motion along her pussy, and against her clit.

"Do you like that?" he murmured, skimming his lips along her damp cheek, feeling her start to shake and unravel as her orgasm approached.

"Yes," she whimpered, her hips canting toward the pressure of the spray. "Oh, God, please…"

He could have easily finished her off just like this, but he was greedy enough to want to make her come with his mouth. Just as she started to tremble, he removed the stream, causing her to cry out in protest, until he kneeled in front of her and replaced the sensation with the heat of his mouth, and the firm lick of his tongue along her slit.

Seemingly lost in pleasure, she slid one of her legs over his shoulder, spreading herself open even more, allowing him complete access to every intimate part of her. She dug her fingers into his hair and angled her hips to better fuck his mouth and tongue, and it was the hottest goddamn thing to watch her become this sensual creature who no longer held anything back.

He ate her like she was dessert, greedily, ravenously. The sinuous way she moved her lower body against his mouth, along with the sexy little sounds that escaped her throat, had his cock throbbing almost painfully. He reached down and wrapped his fingers tight around his length, instinctively stroking his aching dick in a tight grip. The more she writhed and gasped and then sobbed his name, the harder and faster he jerked himself off, until the tension in him was spiraling out of control.

She came with a high-pitched cry, every inch of her shuddering with the force of her release. He groaned against her pussy as his own orgasm slammed into him, driving the air from his lungs as he kept pumping his cock in a tight fist until there was nothing left to spill and the head was too sensitive to touch.

When it was over, they were both gasping for breath.

Georgia tried to stand up on both feet, but her knees seemed to buckle and with a soft laugh she slid down the shower wall until she was sitting on the floor in front of him. She had a sated smile on her flushed face, and when her gaze drifted down to the mess he'd made all over his hand, he gave her a wry grin.

"So much for fucking you on a bed the first time," he said, shaking his head at his lack of control with her.

She bit her bottom lip. "Are we done?"

He chuckled as he picked up the showerhead to rinse them both off, again. "What have I unleashed?" he teased her, then made sure she knew that was just the beginning. "We're not close to being done, but I do need a bit of recovery time."

She exhaled a content sigh. "Well, that was…"

"So fucking hot," he finished for her.

"Yeah." She grinned as he playfully sprayed her breasts with water, her eyes sparkling mischievously as she leaned toward him and kissed him on the lips. "I think I like being bad."

He groaned, because he liked her being bad, too.

Chapter Eight

DREW HADN'T MEANT to fall asleep, but after shower sex with Georgia, they'd gotten into the king-size bed together, she'd cuddled up to his side, and they'd both fallen fast asleep completely naked. No doubt from a combination of the long drive to the cabin, the wine, the hot tub, and of course, mutual orgasms guaranteed to relax them both.

He also didn't expect to wake up the next morning to the arousing sensation of having his cock stroked by someone else's hand, one that was soft and warm and explored his morning hard-on. *Georgia's hand.*

His mind stirred along with his body, and he groaned, letting him know that this seduction wasn't just an erotic dream, but reality. Still, he kept his eyes closed, enjoying the pleasurable sensations coursing through him. He felt a shift beside him on the bed, then lips touching down on his stomach before trailing slow, damp kisses down to join the hand on his dick.

A tongue swiped over the sensitive head, followed by the slide of her thumb, and he shuddered and opened his eyes, staring down at Georgia as she tightened her fist around him, her sultry gaze meeting his.

He reached down, threading his hand through her disheveled hair, loving how mussed she looked, and he'd yet to fully fuck her. "You're quite busy this morning," he murmured.

"I didn't want to let this erection go to waste." She grinned impishly. "Happy birthday to me."

Then she took him into her mouth and sucked him down to the back of her throat. Her lips slid up and down, slow and teasing, again and again. He exhaled a harsh breath as she licked the underside of his cock with her tongue while pumping his length in her slick hand, her eyes closed as if she were enjoying this just as much as he was.

Her mouth was the closest thing to heaven, and as she continued to kiss and suck him, he was unable to stop himself from gripping strands of her hair and slowly thrusting up toward her greedy mouth. With each glide of her lips, his body grew more and more tense. His release rose to the surface, and as much as he appreciated her efforts, he didn't want a repeat of last night. This time when he came, he wanted to be deep inside her pussy.

Tightening his fingers in her hair, he pulled her up, forcing her to release his dick while he still had the willpower to do so. She made a soft sound of protest and glanced up at him with her brows furrowed in disappointment.

"Don't worry, we're not done yet," he promised. "I want you to come up here and ride my cock."

She hesitated, her expression shy and tentative. "I've…umm…never done it that way before."

He was shocked, considering it was such a basic position. "Then you're in for a treat. And so am I."

He helped her move over him and straddle his hips while he slid the tip of his cock through her slick folds, then notched the head at her entrance and eased in an inch. She gasped, her hands coming down to his stomach to brace herself. She was already tight, and feeling her tense up, he gently grabbed her waist to guide her all the way down.

"Relax and let your body adjust while gravity does the rest," he murmured, as her silky heat enveloped his shaft until she was completely impaled on him.

"Now what?" she whispered.

He chuckled at her sweet naivete. "Now, you use my cock however you want. Don't think. Just do whatever feels good." He slid his hands along the indentation of her waist and up to fondle her perfect breasts. "Show me what a dirty girl you can be as you fuck yourself on my cock while I enjoy the view."

She licked her lips, and keeping her hands on his abdomen, she started to slowly move her hips, sliding them back and forth and grinding down, then lifting up slightly so that she could bounce on his shaft. He let her take her time and experiment to find what position felt best, and it didn't take her long before she was gasping and moaning and tossing her head back, her sexy body arching to take more of him while she chased her orgasm.

"Touch yourself," he demanded, knowing that direct stimulation would give her the friction she needed to get off.

Her fingers slid between her spread legs, and he watched as she circled and rubbed her clit and started to pant. She cried out as he pinched her nipples to elevate her pleasure, then slid his hands around to her ass to lift her a few inches so that he could brace his feet on the bed and piston his hips up and down to pound into her.

He fucked her hard, fast and deep, jarring her entire body with each driving thrust. Georgia's internal muscles squeezed around him, eliciting a guttural groan from his chest. She looked incredible on top of him, so out of control and holding nothing back. Her swollen lips parted, her face flushed with desire, and those full breasts jiggled so damn enticingly.

"Do it, Georgia," he ordered in a gruff tone, needing her to get there first. "I want to feel you come all over my cock."

She rubbed her clit harder, faster, while his cock shuttled in and out of her, and soon her entire body began to tremble as her orgasm surged through her. She cried out and went wild as her climax crested, and he felt every one of those rippling sensations along his shaft.

His own release blasted through him, and with a hoarse shout he slammed into her one last time, letting her still pulsing body milk every last bit of his orgasm out of him.

When it was over, she collapsed on top of his chest, both of them trying to catch their breath. He skimmed his hands up and down her back while she recovered, holding her close, their bodies still intimately locked together, while wondering how the hell he was going to walk away from her after this weekend.

He told himself he had no choice. She was the kind of woman who deserved so much more than he could give her. Like his time and attention. Work was his mistress and demanded long hours out, and after Angie, he couldn't expect any woman to adhere to his insane schedule.

He ignored the painful thump in his chest and told himself he had today and tomorrow with Georgia. And he wasn't going to let any of their time go to waste.

AFTER TAKING A shower and getting dressed for the day in a blouse, shorts, and sandals, Georgia followed the savory scent of breakfast to the kitchen and found Drew busy at the stove. They'd showered—separately, so they didn't get distracted again—and he was wearing a T-shirt, cargo shorts, and a pair of Nikes.

He turned around when he heard her enter, a sexy smile on his lips. His own hair was still a bit damp and finger combed away from his handsome features, and his eyes traveled down the length of her, spending extra time checking out her bare legs, even though he'd seen them plenty last night and just a short while ago.

"Morning, beautiful," he said huskily as he turned off the burners before closing the short distance between them.

Before she could reply, he framed her face in his hands. He tipped her head back and kissed her, slow and sweet, making butterflies erupt in her stomach and leaving her breathless with desire by the time he was done with his romantic, sensual greeting.

"Happy birthday," he said, letting his hands drop away from her cheeks and giving the end of her braid a playful tug.

She grinned, feeling lighter than air and more infatuated with Drew than she knew was wise, but decided it was her day to indulge and enjoy how he made her feel. "Yes, very happy indeed."

"Good. Let's get you fed." He turned back to the stove and the three frying pans on top—one with scrambled eggs, another with french toast, and the other with crispy bacon.

She was impressed that he'd made such an elaborate breakfast. Everything smelled amazing, and her stomach rumbled hungrily. "What can I do to help?"

"If you drink coffee, you can make yourself a cup," he said, pointing to the coffee pot and the mug on the counter. "Then, sit at the table and let me wait on you for your birthday."

She did as she was told, not wanting to argue when he seemed truly in his element in the kitchen. She fixed her coffee with sugar and creamer, then took a seat at the nearby table—which was already set with silverware, butter, syrup, and orange juice—and watched him serve up the food.

He set a plate in front of her, noticing that he'd added a berry compote for the french toast. She couldn't remember the last time, if ever, a man cooked for her, and something so special, too.

"Thank you. This looks amazing." She slathered a bit of butter on her french toast, then added a dollop of maple syrup. "You look very comfortable in the kitchen, which is impressive for a bachelor," she teased him.

He shrugged. "You can thank my mom for that. She taught us to cook growing up. Every Saturday, one of us kids was appointed her sous chef in the kitchen," he said, digging into his scrambled eggs. "She always wanted to make sure that her boys knew how to take care of themselves."

"I like your mother already," she said after eating a bite of bacon. "I wish my mother would have been more hands-on that way, but she never had the patience to teach her daughters anything domestic. For as long as I can remember, we had Maggie, our housekeeper, who did most of the cooking. And if she had a night off, then we would go out to eat. I didn't learn to cook until I was in college and living on my own for the first time. Now, I actually enjoy it."

He ate the last of his french toast and took a drink of orange juice before meeting her gaze from across the small table, a teasing grin curving his lips. "So, a very important question for you…how is it that you've never been on top?"

She blinked at him in confusion, then blushed furiously when she realized he was referencing their sexy time in bed this morning. "The few guys I've been with have just been very…vanilla."

"There's vanilla, and then there's flat-out boring," he said with a chuckle. "I'm going to enjoy corrupting you." He waggled his brows at her.

Her entire body warmed at the thought. She was going to enjoy it as well, even if it meant that no other man would ever measure up after her weekend with Drew.

"So, what's the plan for today?" she asked, once they finished their breakfast and the dishes were done.

He ran a finger down the slope of her nose and grinned. "I'm going to test just how daring you can be."

She bit her bottom lip as she followed him out to the car and got into the passenger seat. "I can't decide if that sounds exciting, or ominous."

"Definitely exciting," he said, without giving her a clue as to what he intended. "A complete adrenaline rush that will stimulate you from your head to your toes."

She could think of only one thing that would feel that good. "More orgasms?" she quipped playfully.

His smirk was slow and sexy as he started the vehicle. "I'll reward you with as many orgasms as you like later, if you accept the challenge."

She frowned at him. "You're being so cryptic."

He shrugged. "I don't want to spoil the surprise."

The challenge, she discovered a short while later when they reached their destination at Hunter Mountain, was being strapped into a harness, stepping off a platform, and sliding along a cable sixty feet above the forest floor. *Holy shit.*

She stared up at the zipline attraction in trepidation, her heart beating wildly in her chest. "I...I don't think I can do this." She heard the quiver of fear in her voice.

Drew came up behind her and slid his arms around her waist, holding her tight to his chest. "I *know* you can," he said confidently, his lips near her ear. "If you really don't want to do it, I'm not going to force you, but I can promise if you give it a try, you won't regret it. Once that initial panic wears off and you're soaring in the air, it's fucking exhilarating. Trust me."

She closed her eyes for a moment. Out of everything he'd just said, it was those last two words that gave her the courage to take this chance. Trusting and believing Drew was easy and automatic. He was pushing her boundaries, broadening her horizons, and as much as this extreme adventure terrified her, she also wanted to conquer her fears. She wanted to be impulsive, a little reckless, and a lot fearless. All the things she'd never allowed herself to be in the past.

"Come on, sweetheart," he encouraged gently. "You got this."

She swallowed hard and nodded her agreement, then let him lead her all the way up the tower to the platform, where they could head down the ziplines side by side. They were both strapped into a secure harness, given helmets and gloves to wear, then clipped to the trolley. The guide gave them the safety spiel, and then it was go time.

Beside her on the far end of the platform, Drew gave her a grin and a thumbs-up sign. She treated him to a faint smile in return as he waited for her to go first. Her knees shook, her stomach flip-flopped, and a quick glance down shot terror through her veins.

Refusing to back out now, she sucked in a breath and leaped off the platform, squeezing her eyes shut and screaming at the top of her lungs. She initially plummeted, then seemed to stabilize as she held on for dear life.

"Open your eyes!" she heard Drew shout.

She wanted to please him. Wanted him to be proud of her. She squinted her eyes open, looking ahead for a moment as the wind blew against her face and through her hair. She glided over the trees beneath her and found herself distracted and mesmerized by the breathtaking view of the forest and mountains and streams below. Her anxiety diminished as a shocking thrill swept through her, and by the end of the ride, she was grinning and filled with pure exhilaration.

Once they were both on the ground and unharnessed, Georgia ran to Drew and jumped into his arms. He gave her a hug and spun her around as she laughed happily, feeling more alive than she could ever remember.

"Oh, my God, that was awesome!" she said, when he finally released her. "Let's do it again!"

He grinned and chucked her under her chin. "That's my girl."

My girl. Georgia shivered at his praise and tried not to read too much into those intimate, possessive words.

Hand in hand, they made their way back up to the start of the zipline and went for another ride, this time with Georgia thoroughly enjoying the sensation of flying in the air and the spectacular views. Then they spent the afternoon at Mid-Mountain, exploring the rope bridges and aerial tree platforms, and ate lunch at a local microbrewery before taking a short hike at Kaaterskill Falls.

By the time they returned back to the cabin late Saturday afternoon, Georgia was blissfully exhausted and in need of a shower. Drew let her go first, and after changing into a pair of jeans and a light sweater for the evening, she laid down on the bed to wait for Drew to finish his turn in the bathroom.

With a deep, contented sigh, she closed her eyes, telling herself she was just going to rest for a few minutes...and promptly fell asleep.

Chapter Nine

AFTER A HOT shower, Drew dried off and then wrapped a towel around his waist before stepping into the bedroom, not all that surprised to find Georgia passed out on the bed. He'd worn her out with their fun day in the sun, along with him encouraging her to embrace her adventurous side, which she'd done with gusto once she'd gotten over her initial fears.

The memory made him grin. He loved that he'd been the one to introduce her to new experiences, that she'd trusted him enough to take that initial leap off the zipline platform when he knew how terrified she'd been. And how much she'd loved the wild, exhilarating ride. But then again, he knew that Georgia needed this, the opportunity to be wild and free and enjoy life to the fullest on *her* terms, and no one else's.

He'd had one of the best days he could remember in recent memory. One where he hadn't been absorbed in work, constantly thinking of clients, or mergers and billion-dollar acquisitions. Not to mention the European offer hanging over his head. All of which made him realize just how badly he'd needed that reprieve from his own constant daily grind.

He quietly dressed, then grabbed a lightweight blanket from the living room and brought it back to the bedroom to drape over Georgia. She was sleeping soundly curled up on her side, but he could see the sweet smile on her lips, her soft, pretty features, and the light, adorable smattering of freckles over her nose and cheeks from being out in the sun.

As he stared down at her, Drew felt an odd, protective tug in his chest that he valiantly tried to ignore, one that stirred up wants and needs that had nothing to do with anything sexual. No, those desires swirling around inside of him had an emotional component to them that were dangerous to even contemplate, considering they'd be parting ways tomorrow afternoon.

Exhaling a deep breath, he walked to the front room. Figuring he had at least an hour or two to kill before dinner while she napped, he sat on the sofa and yeah, workaholic that he was, he retrieved a contract he'd brought with him to look over if he had the time. But no matter how hard he tried to focus on the details of the agreement for his client, he couldn't concentrate, and his mind kept drifting back to Georgia.

He couldn't stop thinking about her delightful smiles, her carefree laughter, her bright, awe-filled eyes throughout the day. The silly selfies she'd insisted they take together, the flirting and teasing, and their easy, natural chemistry and connection. It was as though they'd been a couple for months instead of just being together a few days.

Through the front window, he noticed the sun falling over the horizon and dusk settling in, and since he couldn't give the contract in front of him the attention to detail it required, he put it away to work on tomorrow evening. Instead, he decided to make himself useful and start prepping for dinner.

He turned on the outdoor grill to heat, then returned to the kitchen to season the steaks he'd had delivered the day before, then started making a salad. Just when he thought about waking up Georgia, she strolled out of the bedroom, still looking sleepy, her face pink from her day in the sun.

She gave him a contrite look as she joined him in the kitchen. "I'm so sorry for falling asleep on you."

"No apologies necessary," he said, putting the last of the cut-up tomatoes into the salad bowl with the lettuce and other veggies before tossing it all with Italian dressing. "How are you feeling?"

"Much better." She came up beside him as he washed and then dried his hands. "Thank you for today. It was honestly a blast and something I never would have done on my own."

"I'm glad you had a good time." Loose strands of hair had escaped her braid, and he gently brushed them off her cheek, letting his touch linger while meeting, and holding, her gaze. "I wanted to do something memorable for your birthday."

"Memorable, terrifying, and absolutely exhilarating," she said with a laugh. "Best birthday ever. I can't wait to do it again sometime."

His stomach felt as though it had been delivered a gut punch, because some other lucky guy would be the one to take her next time. "I think I've created a thrill seeker."

She gave him an impish grin. "You just might have."

He resisted the urge to pull her into his arms for a kiss, knowing he'd never be able to stop with just one. "Are you hungry for dinner?"

She nodded eagerly. "I'm starved. What can I do to help, and do not tell me to sit and let you wait on me."

Her stern look amused him. "Okay, then how about you set the table while I grill the steaks," he suggested. "Medium good for you?"

"That's perfect."

He left her inside while he cooked the ribeyes on the barbeque, and when he returned, the table was completely set, including two glasses of wine. They ate dinner, and afterward, he insisted she stay seated while he washed the dishes. Then he grabbed a plastic grocery bag with a few items inside, took her hand, and led her to the back patio for one last surprise.

He ignited the wood in the firepit, pulled one of the lounge chairs close and sat down, his legs straddling the chaise to make room for Georgia to settle in between, in front of him. It was a gorgeous, cool evening outside, dark all around them except for the fire and the clear sky above, scattered with a blanket of stars and constellations.

He reached into the plastic grocery bag and pulled out a box of graham crackers, a bag of marshmallows, and bars of chocolate. "So, I know this isn't a traditional birthday dessert, but I thought it would be fun to make s'mores."

She looked at him with a grin, her eyes sparkling in the firelight. "I love that idea! I've never made s'mores before." He couldn't imagine not having experienced the pure joy of marshmallows on sticks, heating them over the campfire, and sandwiching them with chocolate and graham crackers.

Her excitement and pure delight made him smile, and once again, he loved that he was the one to give her this unforgettable experience. "We made them all the time when we came up here for our vacations. So, I'd consider myself a pro," he said in a playful brag. "And I'll show you how to roast your marshmallow without incinerating it in the fire like Tripp always managed to do."

She laughed, and he reached for one of the long metal skewers he'd put out here earlier, handed one to her, and instructed her to spear a marshmallow on the tip of the steel prong. They'd come a long way from camping and sticks, he mused.

"Now, you put it right at the edge of the fire and slowly rotate the rod so that the marshmallow cooks and gets soft and gooey inside but doesn't burn to a crisp," he told her.

They both leaned toward the fire, and he watched

in amusement as Georgia concentrated on roasting the puffed confection just right. When they were toasted light brown and bubbly on the outside, they removed the marshmallows from the heat and he had her hold both skewers while he snapped a graham cracker in half to make two squares, then placed part of a chocolate bar on top, followed by the melting marshmallow, and topped with another cracker to make a sweet, delicious treat.

Georgia bit into hers and moaned as the gooey dessert filled her mouth, the sexy, seductive sound going straight to his dick.

He grinned and arched a brow at her. "I take it you like it?"

She nodded vigorously and licked a smear of melted chocolate from her bottom lip. "Oh, my God. It's so good."

They enjoyed the rest of their s'mores, then settled back on the lounge chair they were sharing, with Georgia between his legs and reclining with her back to his chest. He wrapped his arms around her, and she exhaled a soft sigh. The only sound was the crackling fire as they stared up at all the brilliant stars twinkling in the night sky.

He could get used to this, he thought, and tried not to let himself get too comfortable with Georgia, and having her around, since they'd be parting ways tomorrow.

"Do you know the seven most prominent constellations from both the Northern and Southern

CARLY PHILLIPS & ERIKA WILDE

hemispheres?" he asked, realizing that instead of torturing himself with what he couldn't have, he was sharing yet another personal thing about himself that not many people other than his family knew. Bringing her closer instead of pushing her away.

"Hmm. Can't say that I do."

"They're Ursa Major, Cassiopeia, Orion, Canis Major, Centaurus, Crux, and Carina," he pointed out. "And I can see most of them right now."

She turned her head to look up at him with wide, surprised eyes. "Well, that's impressive. Are you an astronomy nerd?" she teased.

He chuckled. "You could say that. My father was into astronomy, and I was the only one who really took an interest in it as well. So, as a kid, when we were up here, on a clear night he'd get out his telescope and point out all the constellations. I was fascinated by it all."

She threaded her fingers through his, where he'd placed them on her stomach, the touch simple yet intimate. "You sound close to your dad."

"I am," he admitted, and found himself spilling yet another secret. "A few years ago he was diagnosed with colon cancer, which was a huge scare for all of us after what happened with Whitney. But they caught it early enough that it could be treated, and he's now in remission and doing great."

Relief etched her features. "I'm so glad to hear that."

They went back to looking at the night sky, relaxing by the warmth of the fire. After a while, Georgia said, "So, what, exactly, is a constellation?"

Her interest in astronomy surprised him. "It's a group of visible stars that form a perceived pattern or outline that typically represents an animal, mythological subject, or inanimate object."

"Oh, like the Big or Little Dipper?" she asked thoughtfully, her eyes still cast up toward the stratosphere.

Her head rested on his chest, and he absently rubbed his cheek in her fragrant hair. "Actually, the Big Dipper is a grouping of stars within the constellation Ursa Major, which is also known as The Great Bear."

"Show me where it is," she said eagerly.

He directed her toward the Big Dipper, and once she found that pattern, he guided her along the line of stars that outlined the shape of a bear.

"Oh, my God, that's amazing!" Her enthusiasm was genuine and infectious. "Show me another."

Enjoying her interest and excitement, he pointed out Orion, which was identified by his "belt" of stars, and Centaurus, which outlined the shape of half man, half horse.

Georgia was completely enthralled, and as they were discussing the various other constellations, a streak of light shot across the sky.

She gasped and pointed toward the flash. "It's a shooting star!"

He chuckled, not wanting to burst her bubble by

explaining in more technical terms that it was actually tiny bits of dust and rock called meteoroids falling into the earth's atmosphere and burning up. Instead, he indulged her wonder and amazement.

"It's your birthday," he whispered into her ear. "Close your eyes and make a wish."

She did, and after a few silent moments, she blinked her lashes open, then turned around in his arms, smiling up at him. "I—"

"Don't tell me your wish," he said, placing his finger over her parted lips.

He wasn't sure if he was more afraid to hear her deepest desire or if he believed it wouldn't come true if she divulged it, and realized it was the former. He didn't want to listen to her hopes and dreams in case it was something he wished for too, but knew he'd never be able to give her.

"I won't," she said, as he removed his finger. "I just wanted to say that there's one last thing I want for my birthday."

In that moment, he'd literally give her almost anything her heart desired. "And what's that?"

"You," she said simply, her voice lowering to a sultrier pitch. "Meet me in the bedroom in five minutes."

He wasn't about to say no when he didn't want the night to end. Didn't want reality and the outside world to intrude on their perfect bubble.

He helped her up, and when she disappeared into the cabin, he gave her the time she requested while he extinguished the fire pit, then cleaned up the remnants of their s'mores and put the leftover items in the kitchen.

When he finally walked into the bedroom a short while later, his heart slammed in his chest, and his mouth went bone dry at what he found waiting for him...Georgia, kneeling on the bed wearing the red lacy lingerie her sister had given her. The sheer cups barely contained her voluptuous breasts, and the front of the babydoll draped open to tempt and tease him with flashes of pale, smooth skin and the flimsy panties she wore.

With her wavy blonde hair loose and cascading around her shoulders, she looked like a gorgeous vixen. There was no way he could resist her.

He glanced around. Also, set out on the comforter were the items he'd gotten a glimpse of yesterday. A silk blindfold mask, fur-lined handcuffs, and a feather tickler.

When he lifted his gaze back up to her face, he liked what he saw. A woman confident in what she desired. A bad girl who didn't want safe, vanilla sex. An impulsive, daring minx who was beyond ready to take a walk on the wild side with him. And if he'd had something to do with the changes, all the better.

"What do you want, Georgia?" he murmured, slowly moving toward the bed, his cock already straining the front of his jeans.

Her lips parted, and her blue eyes darkened to a deep velvet. "I want you to corrupt me," she said breathlessly, repeating back what he'd told her this morning about how he'd enjoy showing her the more wicked side to sex.

He let his lips lift in a wolfish grin because it would be his pleasure to grant her wish.

✧　✧　✧

VOICING HER DEEPEST desires to Drew was easier than Georgia expected. But then again, if there was any man truly capable of corrupting her in the best way possible, it was the one who'd already pushed her beyond any of her previous sexual encounters.

He made her feel safe. Unashamed. And brazen enough to ask for what she wanted, knowing that he was more than willing to provide that pleasure.

Kneeling on the bed, she licked her lips as she watched Drew advance. The heat in his eyes as he raked them over her curves—highlighted in the sexiest lingerie she'd ever worn—caused her entire body to hum with anticipation. He pulled his Henley off and dropped the shirt to the floor, making her fingers itch to touch his firm chest all the way down to his toned abdomen.

Then he unfastened the top button of his jeans and pulled down the zipper, drawing her gaze to the light dusting of hair that disappeared into the waistband of his boxer briefs as he shucked his pants. Her mouth watered at the sight of his long, thick erection visible beneath the form-fitting fabric.

"Lay back on the bed," he ordered, picking up the

fur-lined handcuffs and looping them through a wooden slat in the headboard. "And put your hands above your head."

The commanding tone of his voice made her warm and weak, flooding her sex with moisture. She assumed the position, lifting her arms so he could shackle her wrists, keeping them restrained. The thought of being at his mercy sent a thrill of excitement through her.

Then, he gently pushed aside the sheer fabric covering her midsection, exposing her stomach, and leaving only her breasts and pussy covered by the red lace. Since she hadn't yet spread her legs, he'd yet to discover that the underwear was crotchless, but he'd find that little surprise soon enough.

Next, he picked up the silk blindfold and slipped the mask over her eyes, taking away her sight so she only had her other senses to rely on. She breathed in deep, inhaling his now familiar masculine scent. She heard him move, not sure where he was until she felt the soft brush of feathers skimming her throat and slowly moving down her chest in a light, teasing caress across her skin. She gasped, the tickling sensation making her nipples tighten into hard peaks against the lacy material.

He leisurely traced the upper swells of her breasts with the plumes, making her nipples throb, then swept the feathers lower, skimming his way down her bare stomach. By the time he reached the waistband of her panties, she was moaning, panting with arousal, and squirming restlessly.

"Open your legs for me," he said gruffly.

She parted her thighs, and the lacy slit along the crotch separated to reveal her pussy, making her wish she could see his face as he discovered the provocative surprise.

She heard him suck in a harsh breath, then released it on a deep, guttural growl. "Fuck me." His voice sounded as though he'd swallowed gravel. "Such a dirty, filthy girl, showing off your pretty pussy like this. You're already so fucking wet for me…I can't wait to get my mouth on you."

She whimpered, hoping that's what she would feel next, but instead, he tickled and tormented her with the soft feathers, swirling them over her sensitive clit until her body shook with need and she was pulling desperately on her restrained arms. The gentle strokes weren't enough friction to get her off, just make her beg and plead and babble incoherently.

"Do you want to come, sweetheart?" he asked, his deep, husky voice near her ear as he trailed the plumes down one thigh and up the other until he reached the apex again, barely touching the feathers against her sex.

She made a frantic sound in the back of her throat and nodded her head eagerly.

"Use your words," he ordered, while his warm, damp lips touched down on her chest and drifted down to her breasts.

"*Please*," she blurted out, her back arching and her

hips moving to chase the soft, agonizing twirl of feathers barely making contact with her throbbing clit. "Please make me come."

"And tell me, how would you like that orgasm, hmm?" he murmured wickedly.

"With your mouth and your tongue…" She cried out as he scraped his teeth across her nipple through the lace covering her breasts, the rough, abrasive sensation sending a jolt of lust through her entire system.

"With my mouth and tongue doing *what*?" he prompted, demanding more.

Beneath her blindfold, she could feel her cheeks blush furiously. Her entire body was on fire at the thought of saying the words he wanted to hear, but her need outweighed any last hesitation. She'd asked him to corrupt her, and she embraced her own power and confidence in this sexual dynamic.

She curled her hands into fists above her head and let the words leave her in a rush. "I want you to lick my pussy and suck my clit until I come."

"That's my good girl," he said, his sexy, seductive praise ramping up her arousal even more.

Suddenly all touch ceased, his mouth and feathers gone, and she whimpered her protest. But then he was on the bed between her legs, spreading her thighs even wider apart, and skimming his lips slowly, sensuously, up to her exposed pussy. She felt his thumbs push aside the lace, and then his mouth was on her, his tongue sliding deep.

She whimpered, quivering with mindless, desperate need as he licked every inch of her and finally sucked her clit. He thrust two fingers inside her core, pumping them in and out in perfect rhythm, and used the flick of his tongue until she had no choice but to surrender to the intensity of the orgasm barreling through her.

She screamed his name and barely had time to recover before he was moving over her and aligning their bodies. His hips forced her legs even wider apart as he settled in between, the smooth, hard tip of his cock poised to drive deep inside her.

He pulled off her mask, finally enabling her to see him, to look at his face and witness the hot, untamable hunger in his eyes. He threaded his fingers in her hair and tugged her head back, making her very aware of how much control he had over her body with her hands still cuffed to the headboard and his weight pressing her into the mattress.

She found it thrilling to be in the throes of his dominant passion, to have been the one to push him to this extreme.

He kept his gaze pinned on hers. "I want you to look at me as I make you mine," he said, the bittersweet words squeezing around her heart before he filled her all the way up with one hard, driving thrust.

She gasped at the shock of being impaled on his cock, desire immediately tightening low in her belly as he began driving harder, deeper into her, as if he were trying to imprint everything about her to memory. She met him thrust for thrust, tilting her hips to deepen the penetration even more.

She felt the exact moment when he reached the end of his tether. With a low, unraveling groan, he slammed his body into hers in one final, deep stroke that claimed her completely. He buried his face against her neck and exhaled in a rush as he tensed and jerked as the last of his orgasm shuddered through him.

Her own pleasure was sublime, eliciting so many overwhelming emotions that surpassed mere attraction to Drew, or even infatuation. What she felt for him, in a very short amount of time, was just as terrifying as jumping off that zipline platform earlier today—but with no safety net to catch her if she fell.

She told herself he'd given her a weekend beyond anything she could have imagined...even if she'd secretly wished for so much more. She'd had so many amazing experiences with him, and no one and nothing could take those memories away.

It wasn't nearly enough.

Chapter Ten

GEORGIA WALKED INTO work the following Monday morning after her weekend with Drew, her emotions an odd, jumbled mixture of happiness and disappointment. She never would have believed she could experience such contradictory feelings at the same time, but there was no separating the two distinct sentiments that had been warring inside of her since Drew had dropped her off yesterday afternoon.

Thinking about her time with him made her smile and was definitely responsible for the light, pleasant sense of happiness bolstering her up. But she'd be lying to herself if she didn't admit that she was saddened by the fact that he'd stayed true to the subtle warning he'd given her at the beginning of their weekend together—that work kept him too busy for him to commit to any kind of relationship.

And he'd backed up that claim by walking her to her apartment and kissing her goodbye, no words necessary for her to know things were over.

From the beginning, she'd known her time with him was temporary—despite the undeniable chemistry and connection that had formed between them. He'd given her the best weekend of her adult life, stirred up her emotions, and now she was going to have to figure out how to get over him and move on.

If that was even possible.

So, as disappointed as she was, she was grateful she hadn't been blindsided when they parted ways without any promises to see one another again. She hadn't asked, not wanting to put him on the spot or risk rejection, and he hadn't suggested another date. She respected his decision and honesty, but that didn't mean the reality of the situation didn't hurt her heart. Which told her just how far and fast she'd fallen for Drew Daniels.

As soon as she entered the office, Billie rushed up to her, a huge, expectant grin on her face. "So, how did your weekend with Drew go?" she asked, her blue eyes filled with curiosity behind her black-framed glasses. "Where did he take you, and what did you do?"

Georgia laughed as her coworker and friend shot off the questions faster than she could answer them.

"The weekend was fantastic," she said, starting toward the break room with Billie following behind, desperate for some caffeine to jump-start her morning. "And he took me to his family's cabin in the Catskill Mountains." As for how they'd spent their time together, she kept her summary PG-rated. "We went ziplining, he made me a steak dinner for my birthday, and we ate s'mores while he gave me a quick rundown of the basic constellations. It was a really fun weekend."

Billie set her hands on her hips and narrowed her gaze while Georgia made herself a cup of coffee from the Keurig. "Why do I get the impression you're skipping over all the good stuff?"

She laughed. "There was definitely good stuff," she admitted, but didn't elaborate. Those memories were for her, and her alone.

Billie settled a hip against the counter, still not done with her interrogation. "Okay, so when are you seeing him again?"

Trying to ignore the twist in her stomach that question evoked, Georgia instead focused on stirring cream and sugar into her coffee. "I, umm, it really was just a weekend thing," she said as casually as she could muster while glancing back at Billie. "You know, him fulfilling his duties of the bachelor auction. He recently made partner at his firm, which doesn't leave him with a lot of time for dating."

Billie's lips pursed in disappointment. "Well, that sucks."

Georgia couldn't agree more with Billie's sentiment, but she refused to allow the situation to depress her. She picked up her mug and they headed back into the reception area of the office just as Aurora walked in the door, doing her best to hold on to a gorgeous bouquet of red roses in a crystal vase with one hand and her purse in the other. Her pregnant belly didn't help matters, and the vase tipped precariously in the crook of her arm.

Billie rushed over to rescue the flowers before they slipped from Aurora's grasp. "Oh, my God! If Nick insists on giving you flowers, the least he can do is have them delivered to the office so you don't have to struggle with them."

Aurora laughed as Billie set the bouquet down on the table near the couch in the reception area. "I would agree, but these aren't for me. They were being delivered to the security desk downstairs when I walked in. The guard told me they were for Georgia, so I offered to bring them up since I was heading to the office anyway."

Georgia's heart skipped a beat, and Billie's brows rose above the frames of her glasses as she turned her gaze to Georgia. "Well, maybe you completely misread the situation."

Had she misinterpreted things? More than anything, Georgia wanted to believe that might be true, and the possibility had her heart beating wildly in her chest.

Billie plucked the envelope that had been tucked into the middle of the roses and handed it to Georgia with a flourish. "Why don't you see what he has to say?"

Unable to contain her growing excitement, Georgia removed the card and read the message that had been written inside.

Georgia, happy belated birthday. I've been thinking of you and would love to take you out to dinner this week. Sincerely, Elliott.

Elliott's unexpected note was like a splash of cold water, immediately dousing her hopes and anticipation that the flowers were from Drew—a definite *womp, womp* kind of moment.

"Who is Elliott?" Billie asked, wrinkling her nose in confusion as she peered at the card from next to Georgia.

Swallowing back her disappointment, she stuffed the card back into the envelope. "He's an attorney who works at my father's firm who has been trying to get me to go out with him."

"I take it you're not interested?" Aurora asked.

"Not in the least, and he's not taking the hints I've been tossing his way." She rubbed her fingers along her forehead and sighed. "It also doesn't help that he works for my father, and my parents think he's a great catch, which puts me right in the middle of an awkward situation."

Aurora winced and absently rubbed a hand over her pregnant belly. "Yeah, that is an uncomfortable position to be in."

But it was also one Georgia needed to address at some point soon, despite how much she hated any kind of conflict or confrontation.

Everyone went their separate ways, and Georgia headed to her own office and sat down at her desk. She took a drink of her now lukewarm coffee, knowing she couldn't ignore the fact that Elliott had sent her the bouquet, and she needed to thank him.

Retrieving her cell phone, she pulled up his number, ever so mindful of not saying anything to offend him. As much as she wanted to tell Elliott to *leave me alone, I'm not interested*, she didn't want to come across as a bitch and have that attitude get back to her father and cause tension or friction between her dad and a man he'd made junior partner at the firm. Or between Georgia and her parents. Because heaven knew, her mother would find out and begin her pressure campaign.

Her stomach twisted in knots as she very politely typed out, **Thank you for the roses. They're beautiful. Unfortunately, I've got a full week and won't be able to make dinner. Thank you for thinking of me, though.**

His reply came well over an hour later, which told Georgia he'd either been busy, or annoyed by her message. Probably the latter, considering the curt tone of his response: **I understand. Maybe another time.**

She should have felt immense relief that she was off the hook, but she knew a persistent man like Elliott wouldn't be so easily discouraged.

As soon as Drew walked into The Back Door, he spotted his brother, Beck, sitting at a high-top table in the bar area of the casual restaurant, their choice of drink already ordered and delivered. Catching sight of Zach Dare, one of the owners of the place, who was also a friend, Drew lifted a hand in greeting as he made his way to Beck.

Drew had received a text a short while ago from his brother, saying he was in the neighborhood and had just parted ways with a client who'd been interested in purchasing a building nearby, and how about they grab a drink and a bite to eat?

Since it was after seven on a Thursday evening and he'd yet to eat dinner, Drew agreed, ready to leave work and relax a bit after a day full of meetings, negotiations, and facilitating a legal due diligence discussion for a client.

He slid onto the stool opposite Beck, and once Drew was settled in, he picked up his glass of bourbon. "Thanks for ordering for me," he said, and took a drink just as one of the waitresses delivered a plate of sliders for each of them.

They dug into their meal, their conversation initially revolving around work—Drew and his current caseload, and Beck with his latest high-end real estate deal. Halfway through eating their burgers, his brother smoothly changed the subject.

"So, Chloe is dying to know how your weekend with Georgia went."

Drew arched a brow and wiped his fingers on a napkin. "Is that the real reason you wanted to meet me for dinner? To get the goods for your wife?"

Beck shrugged. "I really *was* in the area for a client, but yeah, when I called Chloe a while ago to let her know I might be a bit late getting home, she suggested I meet you and find out what happened. I figured you'd rather talk to me than answer her twenty questions," he said with a smirk.

Drew groaned and shook his head. He loved his sister-in-law, but she was way too invested in his love life…or rather, making sure he had one. According to his brother, Chloe just wanted Drew and Tripp to be as deliriously happy as she and Beck were.

"I took her up to the family cabin," Drew told him, and finished off his last slider.

Beck stared at him in surprise. "Well, that's…cozy. I didn't realize Georgia was the outdoorsy type. I would think most women would prefer something more luxurious and upscale than a rustic cabin."

"It was definitely a risk," he admitted. "But we had a great time. I took her to Hunter Mountain and talked her into giving ziplining a try." He felt a pang in his chest as he recalled the fun memory and just how much adventure, in and out of the bedroom, he'd been able to coax out of Georgia.

"Damn," his brother said, sounding impressed. "I can't even get Chloe to give ziplining a try the few times we've been there." He placed his napkin on his empty plate and pushed it aside. "So, you had a great time…and?" he prompted.

He gave his brother a blank look, not sure he wanted to dig deeper into the aftermath of his time together with Georgia. "And what?"

"Come on," Beck said with a groan, calling him out on his vague reply. "You know Chloe is going to want to know details. Like, if you're going to see her again."

Drew did his best to tamp down the dozens of regrets he'd dealt with since parting ways with Georgia. He kept telling himself he'd done the right thing, that he wouldn't lead Georgia on and end up hurting her, but almost five days later, and those reassurances sat like lead in his stomach.

He downed the last of his bourbon and set the glass on the table. "I haven't seen or talked to her since I dropped her off on Sunday."

Beck eyed him knowingly. "Her choice, your choice, or a mutual decision?"

Drew exhaled a deep breath. "Mine."

His brother frowned in confusion. "So, you're telling me things were great, you had a fantastic time with her, and then…you just walked away?" His voice rose in a combination of shock and disappointment.

He already felt shitty enough without his brother pointing out the obvious, especially since Drew had spent the past week thinking about Georgia and resisting the urge to call or text her because he fucking missed her. He'd then remind himself of the reasons why it was smarter to let her go before either of them became more invested and started wanting…more.

"It's just all so fucking complicated," Drew muttered, and scrubbed a hand along in jaw in frustration. "Georgia deserves more than being with a man who works long, endless hours and doesn't have the time to commit to a relationship. I've been down that route, and it didn't end well," he said. "Angie slept with another man because she felt neglected, and that was *before* I made partner." He shook his head. "And to make matters worse, her father's firm is a rival to McKenzie Goodwin."

Beck drummed his fingers on the tabletop in thought, a habit Drew was used to. "Trust me, I get complicated more than most when it comes to wanting a woman I shouldn't," he said, referring to his own initially tumultuous relationship with Chloe, who'd been his ex-best friend's sister and someone who should have been completely off-limits. "Except Chloe is the best thing to ever happen to me. If I was able to work through my issues with her brother so I could be with her, then you could do the same with Georgia's father and deal with any conflict of interest that might arise. It all depends on how much you're willing to sacrifice to be with her."

That was the crux of Drew's problem. He wanted Georgia, *badly*, and that desire hadn't abated one iota since they'd parted ways. All those nuances he'd learned about her at the cabin stayed with him. Her fortitude when it came to taking risks that scared her, her vulnerable side that made him want to protect her—even though he knew she could take care of herself—and just how easy it had been for him to share some of his most personal and intimate life stories with her.

Connecting with her emotionally had been effortless, and she'd brought out a side to him he hadn't known existed...she made him desire something in his life beyond work. Except his greatest fear remained.

Could he balance a demanding job and a relationship without fucking it up?

The sacrifice Beck referenced would be time. Time that Drew would have to carve out of his hectic business schedule and make being with Georgia a priority. Something that would have to be a conscious choice, not an obligation as it had felt like with Angie. He already knew he wanted to try and find a balance that included work and a relationship with Georgia, because the thought of her being with anyone else made him more than a little insane.

"Look," Beck said, cutting into his thoughts and bringing Drew's attention back to his brother. "We've got that barbeque at Mom and Dad's this weekend. It was something you were going to anyway, so why not invite Georgia and see how it goes with her out in the real world?"

Drew blinked. Beck's suggestion was excellent. His weekend with Georgia in the Catskills had been living in a bubble, just the two of them in an intimate setting with no outside influences. Bringing her to the barbeque would give him an idea of what it would be like to truly date her. To see if their chemistry and connection could build into something more solid and real. Something that could weather the demands of his job and other obstacles thrown in their way.

Taking her to spend time with his family, who were the most important people in his life, was a huge deal for Drew. It was a significant step and one he didn't take lightly, but if he was going to try to grow this relationship with Georgia, then he wanted to share that important aspect of his life with her, as well.

He parted ways with Beck a short while later, and as soon as Drew was in his car, he swiped open his cell phone and pulled up Georgia's number, his thumb hovering over the connect button. As confident as he was in his daily life and at work, he couldn't deny feeling apprehensive now.

He'd caught the disappointed look in her eyes when he'd walked her to her door, kissed her cheek, and left without a word about seeing her again. It didn't matter that he'd insinuated he had no time for a relationship. He'd let too many days pass without contacting her in any way. She'd have every right to want to protect herself from being hurt by him again and say no to his invitation.

There was only one way to find out. He tapped her phone number, let the call connect, and waited to see if she'd answer.

AFTER LEAVING WORK for the evening, Georgia drove to Midtown Manhattan to the upscale French restaurant in the city where her mother had made reservations to celebrate Georgia's birthday, since she'd been away the previous weekend with a "friend" as far as her parents knew.

It was Thursday evening, the only night that week when she, her parents, and Courtney had all been free to meet for dinner. Georgia hoped that the next few hours were relaxing and drama free.

A call came through on her car's Bluetooth, the name "Drew Daniels" appearing on the display. Her heart leaped in her chest, and she did her best to tamp down the jolt of excitement that surged through her. She hadn't heard a word from him since he'd dropped her off the previous Sunday, and she couldn't help but be wary of why he was calling now.

She debated letting the call go to her voice mail, but she was too curious about his reason for contacting her, and if she were honest with herself, she wanted to hear his voice.

Exhaling a deep breath to calm her nerves, she connected the call. "Hello?"

"Hey, Georgia," he said, his tone surprisingly tentative. "How are you?"

The question was a loaded one. How was she? Lonely, definitely. Annoyed that he'd consumed so many of her thoughts when she needed to get over him. Frustrated that he hadn't been able to commit beyond their weekend together, even though he'd been honest about his intentions.

Her emotions had run the gamut, so she settled for a generic, neutral, "I'm great." *A blatant lie, but she wasn't about to admit the truth.*

"Good," he replied, and hesitated for a moment before saying, "I'm calling to see if you'd like to go to my parents with me for a barbeque on Sunday."

Georgia was so stunned by the unexpected invitation, she nearly slammed on her brakes in the middle of the street. "Why?" she blurted out.

"Fair question," he acknowledged, considering his previous stance on seeing her again. "Because, quite honestly, I'd like to spend more time with you."

His voice had dropped to a low, husky pitch, laced with the barest of uncertainty. As if he knew what a gamble it was to ask her out and risk her rejection after ending things once his obligatory weekend with her had been over.

When she didn't give him a quick, resounding yes, he swore under his breath. "Okay, maybe I need to grovel a bit more," he muttered.

She grinned to herself, enjoying this humbler side to Drew. "Yes, I think it might help your case if you do."

"Look, I think maybe I was too hasty in ending things between us," he said, his tone gruff. "It was a gut reaction based on my past track record with… relationships. But I can't help but feel like you and I shared something special at the cabin, and I really want to believe that whatever is between us is worth pursuing. I don't want any regrets where you're concerned."

Everything inside of her softened at his heartfelt words, and she could feel herself falling for him even more. "Are you saying you missed me?" she asked softly, flirtatiously.

He laughed, the sound playful and sexy, eliminating the last of anything awkward between them. "Yes, that's implied, but in case you need to hear me say the

CARLY PHILLIPS & ERIKA WILDE

words, I haven't been able to get you out of my mind all week. And if you're going to distract the hell out of me, then I'd like to at least enjoy being with you. So please, say you'll accompany me to my parents on Sunday."

A thrill spiraled through her, even though she told herself not to read too much into the invitation, that it was nothing more than a fun, enjoyable outing. Still, it did involve meeting his family, something no one took lightly. But he wasn't offering a firm commitment or any promises and she still needed to be careful and cautious with her heart.

"Yes, I'd love to go with you," she said, wishing she didn't sound so damn enthusiastic.

"Great."

At last he seemed equally eager to see her again.

They settled on a time for him to pick her up on Sunday just as she turned into the restaurant parking lot and stopped at the valet. They said their goodbyes, and with a pep in her step, she headed into La Grenouille. A text from her mother came through, letting her know that they were already seated, so she gave the host her last name, and the gentleman led her to a table in one of the back rooms.

Her steps slowed, and her stomach pitched when she realized that there was an extra unexpected guest joining the family. Pasting on a smile, she hugged her mother and father, then Courtney, while whispering into her sister's ear, "Why didn't you warn me?"

"And spoil the surprise?" Courtney drawled under

her breath as they released one another, still keeping her voice low. "Actually, I just got here myself and didn't have a chance to send you a text."

Elliott stood behind Georgia, and reluctantly, she turned around to address him. "Hello, Elliott," she said with a cordial smile. "I didn't realize you'd be joining us this evening."

He stepped toward her, kissing her cheek before she could stop him, his lips lingering. "Your mother insisted it be a surprise."

Her mother smiled brightly, as if she'd given Georgia the best gift ever. "When I found out that you told Elliott you were too busy this week to have dinner with him, I thought it was the perfect opportunity to invite him tonight."

Annoyance shot through her. Of course, the fact that she'd turned down Elliott had gotten back to her parents, and she was beyond upset with her mother's interference. If they were in a more private setting, Georgia would have pulled her aside and expressed her displeasure, but considering their very public location in a very expensive, elite restaurant where people came to "see and be seen," she kept her frustration to herself, for now.

They all sat down, with Georgia conveniently seated next to Elliott. For the next hour, while they ate dinner, she pretended to listen to the conversation going on around her, mostly between Elliott and her father as they discussed business. Across the table, her sister made faces at her when no one was watching, and at least Courtney's dramatic eye rolls, nose scrunches, and brow arching managed to add some kind of levity to the situation.

While they ate a delicious chocolate mousse dessert, Georgia opened the presents from her parents— her favorite perfume gift set and a designer wallet she'd been coveting. Then, Elliott reached below the table and handed her a very iconic robin's egg blue gift bag with the name Tiffany & Co stamped across the front. Reluctantly, and very aware that all eyes were on her, she accepted the gift.

"Happy birthday, Georgia," Elliott said, looking pleased with himself. "Your mother assured me that Tiffany's is one of your favorite stores."

She nodded mutely, not sure what to say as she caught her sister's big, wide eyes from across the table that conveyed a "holy shit" message, which Georgia would have found comical if she hadn't been so panicked about what was inside.

She pulled out the small, flat square box, removed the ribbon, and lifted the lid, relieved to find a bracelet and not something more personal, like a ring. The bangle was simple and dainty, exactly something she'd wear, and she had to admit that Elliott had great taste when it came to jewelry.

Normally, she'd be thrilled to receive such a present, but coming from Elliott, it felt...wrong. There was no way she could keep the gift, because she was sure there were certain expectations attached, and she didn't want to give Elliott the impression that it meant anything in terms of the two of them being together in any way. The last thing she'd ever want was to mislead him into believing she was attracted to him. Even a little bit.

She murmured a quiet "thank you" while her mother gushed over the bracelet, her father slapped Elliott on the back in a "good job" gesture, and Courtney cringed in commiseration.

Georgia's stomach churned with anxiety. She couldn't keep doing this. Pretending that this situation with Elliott was okay. Being blindsided by her mother's meddling. Allowing Elliott to think he stood any kind of chance with her. Not because Georgia was only interested in Drew, but she and Elliott had nothing in common beyond him working for her father's firm, and never would. That she knew with certainty.

It didn't matter that her parents were hoping for "more", that having Elliott marry Georgia would ensure that her father's firm remained in the family. That wasn't her burden to carry.

Once her father paid the bill and it was time to go, Georgia lightly touched Elliott's arm to get his attention. "Do you think you and I can go to the bar, just the two of us?"

Judging by the excitement that lit Elliott's eyes, she belatedly realized that invitation sounded way more intimate than she meant it to. "Yes, of course," he said, much too eagerly.

She and Elliott parted ways with Courtney and her

parents, her mother beaming over the fact that Georgia was spending what she believed was quality time with Elliott.

She allowed Elliott to escort her to the lounge, and she directed him to a table off to the side, where it was more secluded and quieter than the main bar area.

Before the bar waitress could come over and take an order for a drink that Georgia didn't want, she got right to the point of meeting with Elliott privately. "As much as I appreciate you thinking of me on my birthday, I can't accept your gift," she said, setting the blue bag on the table between them. "It's too much."

"Too much?" he repeated, frowning at her in confusion. "And here I thought it might not be enough."

She shook her head, not wanting him to misunderstand any part of this conversation. "It's too...intimate, Elliott. You give jewelry like this to someone who means something to you."

He looked affronted. "Of course you mean something to me."

She sighed in exasperation. "You don't even know me. Not really."

His lips thinned in annoyance. "Maybe that's because you haven't given me a fair chance. Are you seeing someone else?" he asked tersely.

"It doesn't matter if I am. This is about you and me, and the fact that I have no romantic feelings for you." She'd tried to let him down gently, but he refused to accept her words or take the hint, leaving her with no choice but to lay things out in a way he couldn't misinterpret.

His gaze narrowed perceptively. "It's Drew Daniels, isn't it?"

She was startled by the anger in his tone, but held firm. "No matter what is going on in my personal, private life, *this* isn't going to work," she said, pointing back and forth between the two of them. "Not now, not ever. I'm sorry if my parents led you to believe otherwise."

Georgia stood up, and before he could respond, she quickly said, "Have a good night, Elliott," and walked out of the lounge without looking back.

Relief poured through her as she stepped outside and breathed in fresh air. She couldn't deny how good it felt to be assertive and put a distinct end to Elliott's interest in her. There was nothing in their conversation that left any kind of opening for him to continue his pursuit, though she had no doubt that she'd still have to deal with her parents at some point soon.

Her mother wasn't one to let something go that *she* wanted, but Georgia was done conforming to her parents' expectations. And if that meant an argument and standing up for herself, she was more than prepared to do so.

Chapter Eleven

GEORGIA STARED OUT the passenger window of Drew's car and rubbed her palms along the skirt of her dress as he turned into a middle-income neighborhood and drove down a tree-lined street toward his parents' house. As hard as she tried, she couldn't stifle the bit of anxiety swirling in her stomach at the thought of meeting his family for the first time.

Drew grabbed her hand and laced their fingers, keeping her from repeating the action once again. "That's the third time you've done that," he said, his tone amused. "Are you nervous?"

She turned and looked at him, biting her bottom lip, which drew his gaze to her mouth. "Maybe. A little," she admitted sheepishly. "It's always a little nerve-racking meeting someone's family. I just want to make a good impression."

He gave her a reassuring smile. "My parents are so down to earth and easygoing. Just be yourself, and I promise they will love you."

With his free hand on the steering wheel, Drew brought the car to a stop along a curb in front of a well-kept house that was beautifully landscaped with greenery and planted flowers. He turned off the ignition and then leaned across the console. The hand that had been holding hers lifted and curled around the back of her neck, and she watched as one of those slow, sinful grins curved his lips.

"There's something I've been dying to do since the moment you opened the door at your apartment," he murmured in a low, husky tone. "But I knew if I dared to kiss you, we'd never make it to my parents because all I would be able to think about is stripping you naked and having my way with you."

She shivered as his thumb brushed along her jawline. "I wouldn't have said no." In fact, she'd been disappointed that he'd been such a gentleman when he'd picked her up.

His eyes darkened at her honest admission. "Which is exactly why I didn't do it."

"And now?" she teased breathlessly.

"Now I want a taste to hold me over until I take you home later." His fingers tightened at the nape of her neck as he brought her mouth to his, their lips barely touching, which only served to increase her anticipation. "But once we're alone later tonight, I'm going to fucking ravish you, and do things to you that will make you blush."

She didn't doubt that at all. "That's quite the claim," she whispered against his lips.

"I assure you, it's a *promise*," he said, then finally kissed her properly, until she was undeniably aroused and moaning at the pure pleasure of connecting with

Drew again, when she thought she'd never get another chance.

When he finished, there was a smug look on his handsome face as his heavy-lidded gaze took in her expression. "Anxiety gone?" he asked.

So, that had been his clever angle, to distract her with a kiss. "Yes, but now I'm hyperaware of *you*."

He smirked a bit arrogantly. "As you should be."

An unexpected smacking sound on the passenger side window startled Georgia, making her jump in her seat.

"Uncle Dew!" a little girl's voice said on the other side, clearly unable to pronounce the "r" in Drew's name. "Open up!"

Drew chuckled and moved back to his side of the car. "That would be my sassy, demanding, adorable niece, Whitney."

They both got out of the vehicle, with Whitney jumping up and down in excitement and her big, wide eyes glued to Drew as he rounded the back of the car. Behind the toddler, Beck and Chloe crossed the lawn to join them, and as soon as Drew reached the sidewalk, he scooped up the little girl and tossed her into the air. Whitney let out a high pitch squeal, and when he caught her again, Whitney smacked a noisy kiss on his cheek.

Clearly, the little girl idolized her uncle, and judging by the smile on Drew's face, he was equally smitten with his niece.

After Georgia greeted the couple, and they did the

same, Drew glanced at Beck, then Chloe. "I wasn't expecting such a boisterous welcome out here on the front lawn, instead of *inside* the house," he said pointedly.

"That's your own fault," his sister-in-law said with a cheeky grin. "Whitney saw you drive up and was getting impatient waiting for you to get out of your car and decided to come and get you."

"I sure am glad your windows are tinted," Beck chimed in with a fabricated scowl. "Wouldn't want to have to explain to my impressionable daughter what you were doing just now."

Drew shrugged and bounced Whitney in the crook of his arm, eliciting a joyful giggle from her. "Georgia and I were just talking."

"Yeah, okay," Beck drawled, his tone now amused. "In that case, you might want to wipe off that bit of pale pink sparkle on your lips."

Georgia's face warmed. She hadn't worn a heavy lipstick today, just a balm with a faint hint of color that had rubbed off on Drew during their kiss.

"Ahh, shit," Drew said, and wiped the back of his hand across his mouth.

"Bad word, Uncle Dew!" Whitney said, poking him in the chest with her little finger.

Drew winced at the cute reprimand. "You're right, Whit. I'm sorry."

Whitney's grin was filled with delight. "Give Mommy a dollar for the swear jar."

He set his niece back on her feet, then dutifully

pulled out his wallet. "Why does she sound *way* too gleeful about that?"

"Because she's saving up for a pony," Beck told him with an eye roll that only the adults could see. "And trust me when I say I've more than contributed my fair share to the swear jar."

Drew opened his wallet and pulled out a twenty-dollar bill, and handed over the payment to Chloe. "I don't have any ones, so this should cover me for nineteen more swear words," he said wryly.

Once the money exchange was made, Georgia gently touched Drew's arm to get his attention. "We need to get a few things out of the trunk before we head inside," she reminded him.

He nodded, and she followed him to the back of the car, where she retrieved a cake carrier with the dessert she'd made, along with a gift bag printed with pastel flowers and butterflies, and pink tissue paper inside. They headed into the house, where Georgia met Drew's mother, Audrey, and his father, Kurt, both who immediately made her feel welcome. Kurt, now a cancer survivor she'd learned from Drew, looked incredibly fit and healthy.

In the kitchen, Georgia set the cake carrier on the counter but held on to the gift bag. "I hope you don't mind, but I wanted to bring something, so I made a dessert. It's a salted caramel chocolate cake."

"Oh, I don't mind at all," Kurt said, and everyone laughed and agreed that there was no such thing as too many desserts.

Whitney tugged on Georgia's dress, and when she glanced down at the little girl, she was eyeing the gift bag curiously.

"What's that?" Whitney asked, pointing to the bag.

Georgia smiled and handed her the gift she'd purchased as a way to break the ice between herself and the young girl. "Well, this is something for you."

"For me?" A cute little frown furrowed between Whitney's brows. "But it's not my birfday," she said, struggling to say the last word correctly.

Unable to resist, Georgia gently smoothed her hand over Whitney's soft head of curls. "I know, but I saw this at the store and thought that if I was a little girl, I would love to have this to play with."

Georgia caught Drew's warm gaze and his appreciative smile as Whitney settled on her knees on the kitchen floor and eagerly tore into the gift while everyone watched. When she saw what was inside, she gasped dramatically.

"Look, Mommy!" she squealed in excitement, lifting the box for everyone to see, which showed a picture on the front of a little girl creating a flower garden from colorful plastic pieces. "I can make my own flowers and garden just like Gamma's outside!"

"Wow, that's so neat," Chloe said, smiling at her daughter. "Why don't you take it out back with Papa, Daddy, and Uncle Drew, and put it together while we're getting things ready for dinner?"

"Okay!" She started to race for the slider leading to the back patio, but Chloe quickly stopped her.

"Whitney, what do you say?" Chloe reminded her.

Whitney glanced back at Georgia, a sheepish look on her face. "Tank you," she said.

"You're welcome," Georgia replied with a smile. "Have fun building your garden."

Whitney continued outside and sat down at the frosted glass-topped table on the patio, where she could be seen from the kitchen. While she waited for the guys to join her, she opened the box and began pulling out various plastic pieces that resembled flowers and leaves and stems.

"So, where is Tripp?" Drew asked of their missing sibling.

"He switched on-call shifts with one of his partners," Audrey said, stirring something that was simmering on the stove. "He was planning on being here but called a short while ago to let me know he wasn't going to make it today, because he was handling a patient that was in respiratory distress from a severe asthma attack."

Drew nodded in understanding. "I haven't talked to him since the night of the bachelor auction," he said, leaning casually against the kitchen island and crossing his arms over his chest. "What's going on between him and the woman who won him? The one he was talking to that night right before the auction. Skye, right?"

"Yes, she won him," Chloe said, pouring three glasses of wine and handing one to her mother-in-law, and the other to Georgia.

Drew frowned, as if he was trying to figure things out with his brother. "Who's got the scoop about what's going on between the two of them? Because clearly, something is going on."

Beck shrugged as he went to the refrigerator and retrieved three bottles of beer for the men. "Only Tripp knows, and I haven't been able to get ahold of him to get any details."

"Well, you all can discuss Tripp's mysterious woman outside while you fire up the barbeque to grill the chicken and ribs," Audrey said, shooing the three men toward the sliding glass door with her hands. "There are too many people in my kitchen, and us girls need room to finish making our side dishes."

Georgia caught Drew's gaze from across the counter, along with the way he raised his brow, silently asking her if she'd be okay if he headed outdoors with his brother and dad, while she stayed inside. She gave him a slight nod and reassuring smile, and once he was gone, she turned back to Audrey and Chloe.

"What can I do to help?" she asked, needing something to do.

"I'm just finishing up the cream corn, but you can cut up the strawberries for the fruit salad," Audrey suggested, pointing to a bowl filled with other fruit and a cutting board with a knife.

"Okay." After taking a drink of her wine, Georgia went to work slicing the berries.

"I have to say it's so nice to have another woman in the fold to balance out the male-to-female ratio in this house," Chloe said light-heartedly, as she set a big bowl of potato salad on the island, then went to a cupboard to retrieve plates, completely comfortable in Audrey's kitchen. "When Tripp is here, it makes for even more testosterone, and it's so not fair."

"I wouldn't consider myself part of the fold," she said with a laugh. "Drew and I are just casually dating." It was the truth, but those words still caused something in her stomach to twist uncomfortably. As much as she'd accepted the parameters he'd set, it was hard not to wish for...more.

Audrey met Georgia's gaze and smiled. "Drew doesn't bring casual dates to family get-togethers, and it's been years since he's brought anyone to meet us, or let us meet them," she said as she turned off the burner to the stove. "So that tells me you're special. Honestly, I'm just thrilled to see him do more than just focusing on work all the time."

Georgia tried not to home in on the word "special" and instead addressed Drew's job as she tossed all the fruit together with two large spoons. "I understand his hectic work schedule, probably more than most people. My father is also an attorney, so I grew up with him spending many evenings and weekends at the office."

"Still, it's good to have more than just work in your life," Audrey said as she brought a platter of ribs and chicken out to the barbeque. "Even Beck has cut back on all the hours and late nights he used to work, hasn't he, Chloe?"

Chloe gave Georgia a commiserating look, one that told Georgia she understood those workaholic tendencies. "Yes, but to be fair, Beck *still* works long hours and late nights when needed, but he brings work home instead of staying at the office, so we do see him more."

"Exactly," Audrey said with a nod, as if that made perfect sense.

"Drew doesn't have a reason to work at home like Beck does," Chloe clarified to her mother-in-law as she placed more side dishes on the counter. "So that's why Drew spends all his time at the office."

"He doesn't have a reason to work at home, *yet*," Audrey pointed out, then gave Georgia a hopeful smile. "Maybe you can change that."

Georgia quickly shook her head. "I'm not changing anything about Drew," she said in a nice, but firm tone.

It wasn't her place to make demands, not even if their relationship were to evolve into something more serious. Any adjustments Drew made to his work life had to be something he wanted, because ultimatums would just breed resentment.

She'd seen that dynamic between her own parents over the years, the times her mother complained about the long hours Georgia's father spent at work and the arguments that ensued that left him feeling guilty and more apt to remain at the office rather than be at home with a harping wife. However, Georgia knew that her mother wouldn't have wanted him to cut back if it meant less money coming in and a change in the lifestyle she was accustomed to, so those demands had always seemed so selfish to Georgia.

Growing up, she remembered her father being at any important event in their lives and the celebrations that mattered most. She'd never felt neglected because of her father's work schedule, like her mother did. Now that Georgia was older and her father was nearing retirement, he'd definitely cut back, but that had been a conscious choice on his part.

As she, Chloe, and Audrey finished prepping the side dishes, all the while chatting, Drew's father began grilling the meat. Georgia set a plate of biscuits on the dining table and glanced out the glass slider, catching sight of Beck and Drew sitting at the table with Whitney, who'd already put together a good portion of her plastic flower garden, her brows knit in concentration as she snapped pieces together.

The two men were talking and occasionally laughing about something, but Drew seemed to be splitting his time between conversing with Beck, and giving Whitney his attention when she formed a flower and wanted him to look at what she'd created. Then, he focused on the little girl, smiling and praising her, his affection for her obvious.

When dinner was served and they were all sitting around the dining room table, Georgia experienced the full scope of Drew's family. She loved how close they were, how easily they all interacted and joked around, parents included. There was no tension here, like she normally felt around her mother. No expectations, either. Just unconditional acceptance and a strong bond between all of them that she envied.

Amidst the loud conversation, the teasing, and laughter, she wondered what it would be like to be a part of this family. To be embraced so completely, to enjoy going to a family dinner instead of dreading the drama that would undoubtedly arise.

As much as she'd enjoyed this day with Drew and his family, it only made her more aware of everything missing in hers.

Chapter Twelve

AFTER DINNER, DREW grabbed Georgia's hand before she drifted off to the kitchen and started helping Chloe and his mother with cleaning up. She glanced at him in surprise and didn't argue when he led her out to the back patio. Everyone else was inside, including his brother and dad, who were in the den watching TV, with Whitney still working on her flower garden on the floor at their feet.

"What's this all about?" Georgia asked as he brought her to the wooden railing overlooking the backyard, which included a quarter acre of land that butted up against a small forest.

He turned toward her, brushing away strands of hair from her cheek. "I haven't had any time alone with you since we got here." And it had been harder than he'd imagined watching her from afar, but also enjoyable, too, to see her interact with his family so well.

She laughed lightly. "That wasn't the point of visiting your family today," she said logically. "We'll have plenty of alone time together later."

She was smiling, but there was something in her

156

JUST A LITTLE SECRET

eyes, a vulnerability he recognized because he'd seen it before. It was shocking to realize just how in tune he was with her emotions, considering the short amount of time he'd known her.

"Are you doing okay?" he asked, unable to keep the concern from his voice. "You got kind of quiet at the end of dinner."

"I'm good," she said, probably to appease him, and followed that up with, "Do you know how lucky you are to have a family like this?"

"I do." And he really did.

Growing up, he'd seen how many of his friends had come from fractured families in one way or another, and he'd always felt safe and secure in the stability his parents had provided, even when the death of Whitney could have torn them all apart.

"Good," she said softly. "Don't take it for grant-ed."

He tipped his head curiously. "Where is this all coming from?"

She shook her head and leaned her arm on the railing. "It's just a comparison of your family versus mine, and really realizing how polar opposite they are. Your parents are so…accepting, and mine, well, especially my mother, have spent most of my life manipulating me into what *they* want me to be. Including setting me up with Elliott Eastman with the hopes that something more would come of it."

For a moment, Drew felt as though someone had just punched him in the stomach, and he couldn't breathe. He'd known the night of the banquet that something was going on between Georgia and Elliott, but had dismissed his gut feeling when she'd told him Elliott wasn't her boyfriend. He believed her, even now, but that didn't mean she wasn't *seeing* him, especially when Drew hadn't discussed them being exclusive. She would have had every right to go out with another man...which, shockingly, had him rethinking their "casual" dating status. The thought of any guy encroaching on what he was beginning to think of as *his* made him want to make a claim on Georgia, here and now.

He shook off those possessive, jealous feelings and forced himself to ask the question foremost in his mind. "What do you mean, setting you up with Elliott? Are you dating him?"

She looked at him with a horrified expression. "Oh, my God, no," she said adamantly, and his relief was immense. "Elliott's been pursuing *me*, even though I haven't been receptive to any of his attempts, and I've tried nicely to turn him down. Since being nice wasn't working, with him or with my parents, when they invited him to my family birthday dinner, I pulled him aside and was more direct. I left no doubt there was nothing between us and never would be." She drew a deep breath. "But now, I need to make it clear to my parents that it's over..."

Now that he knew she wasn't dating the man, Drew thought he'd relax, but he was still tense, knowing her parents wanted another man in her life. He didn't have time to focus on his own proprietary feelings for Georgia because the flash of anxiety he saw in her eyes told him things weren't that simple.

Recalling how difficult she'd found it to take her own college and career path, he thought he understood. "You're worried about upsetting them again?" he guessed.

She glanced out across the yard for a moment, exhaled a deep breath, then met his gaze again. "If only it were that simple," she murmured. "I told you I put my foot down and didn't go to law school. What I didn't tell you was that shortly after I made that announcement and changed my major, my father had a heart attack and triple bypass, which my mother insisted was brought on by stress, meaning *me* defying their wishes and making my father worry about what would happen to the firm when he retired. She told me that if I hadn't been so selfish, it never would have happened."

Anger boiled through Drew's veins on Georgia's behalf, and it took effort not to say some choice words about her mother's emotional blackmail. Instead, he grabbed Georgia's hand and gave it a comforting squeeze. "You're not responsible for your father having a heart attack."

"Logically, I know that," she assured him, and sighed. "But I've always been the good girl in the family. The daughter who fell in line and my parents could count on. And the one time I really defied them for something that meant everything to me, it was like my rebellion came back to haunt me. So, now my parents are focused on Elliott, insisting that we'd be a perfect match and how great would it be if we ended up together and the law firm could stay in the family, like they'd hoped."

"You'd never be happy with a man like Elliott," Drew said, his tone harsher than he'd intended. He wasn't making the claim out of petty jealousy because of his own tumultuous past with the man, but because he knew without a shadow of a doubt that Georgia would wither away with someone as self-centered as Elliott, not flourish like she was meant to.

"Trust me, I knew that the first time I met Elliott. The man's ego is enormous." She shook her head in distaste. "I'm not sure why my parents don't see that side of him."

"Some people are good at hiding those narcissistic tendencies around people they want to impress, like Elliott with your father," Drew guessed.

"I just wish they wouldn't meddle in my life. I'm an adult," she said, her lips pursing in frustration. "I refuse to live my life attempting to live up to their expectations any longer. Which means letting them know they need to stop pushing Elliott on me at family dinners, and stop pulling him into my orbit, for good." She stood up straighter and lifted her chin, a newfound determination glimmering in her eyes. "I hate confrontation and causing conflict and I'm dreading this conversation, but it has to happen."

That show of fortitude impressed him. She was so

much stronger than she realized, and confronting her parents would definitely be the first step in seeing that tenacity within herself, and believing in it.

He reached out and gently skimmed his thumb along her jaw, his gaze holding hers. "Whatever happens, I'm here for you."

It wasn't a declaration or even a promise of more, which he knew he couldn't make right now when he had a huge decision to make at work, and about his busy life in general. But he wanted to be her safe space, that person she knew would support her unconditionally in all things.

"Thank you," she whispered, her eyes filled with that same gratitude.

She placed a hand on his chest, leaning into him with her mouth tipped toward his for a kiss. But before their lips could touch, the sound of the sliding glass door opening made her jerk back, her eyes going wide at almost getting caught.

"It's cake time!" Whitney announced in an excited, singsong voice. "Come and get it!"

Drew chuckled at his niece's enthusiasm. "Come on," he said, taking Georgia's hand and leading her across the patio. "Cake makes everything better."

She laughed. "Yes, it does," she agreed, her angst seemingly gone for now as she followed him inside.

GEORGIA DECIDED ON the drive home that she didn't

want to dwell on anything negative, like her upcoming conversation with her parents. The only thing she wanted to think about was the way that Drew made her feel. Empowered. Heard. Understood. Things that built her up instead of tearing her down with judgment and criticism.

He also made her feel sexy and desired, and that's what she decided to focus on for the rest of the night.

As soon as they entered her apartment, she tossed her purse onto a side table and kissed Drew with a heat and passion he enthusiastically returned, while pulling the shirt from the waistband of his jeans and nearly tearing it off his body in her haste to get him naked as soon as possible.

Wild and reckless, she raked her fingernails along his bare chest and abdomen on her trek down to the front of his pants. She popped open the button and whimpered in frustration as she struggled to pull the zipper over the stiff erection already straining against the denim.

His deep groan vibrated against her lips, and he grabbed her wrists, pulling her hands away. He lifted his mouth from hers and stared down at her, breathing hard. "Whoa, slow down, Tiger," he rasped.

She shook her head, and since he held her hands hostage so she couldn't touch him, she nipped his bottom lip with her teeth. "I don't want anything about tonight to be slow."

His eyes darkened, full of wicked intent. "What are you in the mood for?"

"I need fast, rough, mindless sex."

The bold, brazen words made her face heat, but even as she stated her desires, she knew it wouldn't be mindless. She was too acutely aware of Drew—the masculine scent of him, his strength, and the way she went up in flames wherever he touched her. But *he* didn't need to know how deeply she felt for him, not when she had no idea where his own feelings stood with her.

"I want you to ravish me and do things to me that will make me blush, just like you promised earlier."

Understanding passed across his features, as if he knew she needed to lose herself in pleasure after their earlier emotional conversation. "I can do that."

Swiftly—and with little finesse—he stripped off her dress and the rest of her clothes while guiding her back toward the couch. He took control, giving her no choice but to let him choreograph all aspects of this seduction. When she was completely naked, he pushed her down so that she was sitting on the sofa cushion, then made equally quick work of removing his own clothes.

He didn't give her much time to admire his thick, erect cock before he dropped to his knees in front of her. With his hands on her thighs, he spread her legs indecently wide, licking his lips while staring with hooded eyes at her bare sex, already slick with arousal for him.

"You don't have to—"

"I know I don't *have to*," he growled, cutting her

off as he adjusted her legs over his shoulders and skimmed his hands over her hips as he placed wet, biting kisses up her thighs that would undoubtedly leave marks on her skin. "I want to make you come the first time with my mouth and tongue before I fuck you with my cock. And don't worry, *nothing* about this will be slow."

He didn't lie. The man was driven, his sole purpose to wring an orgasm out of her in the most erotic way possible. She gasped as he devoured her with his mouth, his tongue thrusting deeply before licking his way up to her aching clit. And that's where he stayed, his intimate kiss hot and hungry and so all-consuming she couldn't think straight.

Panting for breath, she tangled her fingers in his hair as he slid his hands up her body until he reached her breasts. He wasn't gentle, and the way he grabbed and squeezed the mounds, then pinched her stiff nipples, shot an electric jolt of heat straight down to her clit. He sucked that bud of flesh harder, and there was no stopping the orgasm that crashed through her.

She cried out, writhing against his mouth as pure bliss saturated her senses.

He didn't give her any time to recover, and she found herself on her knees in front of him on the floor, her upper body braced against the sofa cushion. His hands grabbed her hips, angling them so that the head of his cock had a straight shot into her pussy. Without warning, he slammed into her from behind, filling her to the brim and stealing the breath from her lungs.

He took her...fast...rough...and deep. Oh, God, *so, so deliciously deep.* In this position, she felt impaled to the hilt every time he drove into her with quick, rapid thrusts. With his body pressing her into the couch cushions and holding her down, all she could do was let him use her for his pleasure.

It was exactly what she wanted. Exactly what she needed.

One of his big, warm hands came up, settling at her throat, anchoring her to him even more. He exerted just enough pressure to elicit an erotic thrill and make her eyes roll back at his dominance. She gave herself over to him completely, her body, and even pieces of her heart she knew she'd never get back, no matter how things turned out between the two of them.

"Can't get enough of you," he groaned in her ear as he continued to drive into her without an ounce of control holding him back.

She didn't want him to.

His free hand slid between her legs, finding her sensitive clit and rubbing rhythmically. "Come for me, Georgia," he said, his voice low and deep and demanding.

Desire tightened inside her at his command. Her back arched, and she closed her eyes as the tension inside her became almost unbearable. Then she was awash with pleasure, her body rippling, her muscles tightening around him again and again as she cried out his name. She felt him thrust up into her once, twice, three more times, then shudder as he came deep inside her.

Breathing hard, he wrapped his arms around her and drew her down to the floor to lie across his chest as they both recovered from the adrenaline rush.

Drew had given her exactly what she needed tonight, and even though Georgia didn't know what the future held for them, for now, she was right where she wanted to be. In Drew Daniels' arms.

Chapter Thirteen

GEORGIA DIDN'T HAVE a chance to talk to her parents until the following Friday after work. Between her mother's evening charity commitments, her weekly Mahjong group get-togethers, as well as a gallery event she'd attended, Nina Brooks' social calendar had been full until now.

Of course, Georgia had received a few terse voice and text messages from her mother wanting to discuss her *break up* with Elliott, but that conversation wasn't one she wanted to have over the phone. It was pathetic that a grown man had gone running to her father to tattle on Georgia for ending things. Elliott was *that* desperate to be given the reins of her father's law firm through his daughter.

Beyond ready to get this conversation over with, Georgia texted her mother to find out what evening would be best to stop by the house to talk.

Tonight was the night, and as she pulled into her parents' driveway, she was surprised by her lack of anxiety about confronting them. Instead, determination filled her, and she embraced the feeling, knowing she had Drew to thank for her bravery. She'd learned it was okay to go after what she wanted for a change and though she believed she would have had this conversation with her parents regardless, because she had zero interest in Elliott, having Drew in her corner supporting her, even silently, meant the world to her.

Unfortunately, she hadn't seen him since the barbeque on Sunday. He'd spent the week putting in long hours negotiating a multi-million-dollar merger for a client, and she'd been equally busy at work handling a social media influencer campaign for Future Fast Track. But they'd managed to talk on the phone in the evenings and texted during the day. Light and flirty conversations, and even more serious, emotional ones that gave her deeper insight into the man.

As much as falling for Drew scared her because he'd still given her no promises, it was too late to stop the freefall because her heart was already one hundred percent involved. If she'd thought she'd been in love in the past, she now knew that feeling was nothing compared to the deep connection she had with Drew. One that allowed her to share her fears and insecurities because he'd already proven she could trust him with her deepest vulnerabilities.

There was no doubt in her mind that Drew cared for her, but she also felt him holding back, and all she could do was hope that eventually he'd give them the chance they deserved for a future. At least she had plans with him this coming Sunday, a fun date that she'd set up and a way for her to show how much she appreciated *him*.

Exhaling a deep breath, and ready to get this conversation over with, Georgia got out of her car and made her way inside her parents' house. She found her mother sitting at the kitchen table, drinking a glass of wine, clearly waiting for her to arrive.

The rest of the house was quiet, and she realized she hadn't seen her father's car parked in the driveway.

"Where's Dad?" she asked, setting her purse on the table and taking a seat across from her mother.

Her mother waved a hand in the air, her lips pursed in annoyance. "He was supposed to be here. I told him how important it was that we discussed your recent *choices* together, but a client flew in from Los Angeles last minute and wanted to take your father to dinner, so he won't be home for a few hours."

The resentment in her mother's tone was unmistakable, and a part of Georgia wondered if her father had purposely found a way to avoid this meeting. Yes, he spoke highly of Elliott, but he'd never overtly pressured Georgia into dating the man—that had been her mother's doing. As had been the guilt her mother had heaped upon Georgia when she'd made the decision not to go to law school and instead changed her major, then took a job at a non-profit.

Naturally, her father had been disappointed with her choice since he'd always wanted the firm to stay in the family, but her *mother* never let Georgia forget how much she'd let them down.

The more Georgia thought about things, the more she realized that the manipulation and blame had all come from her mother, even if she'd made it seem like her parents were a united front.

Georgia was beginning to realize that wasn't the case.

"So, let's just get to the point," her mother said in a terse tone. "From what I heard, you embarrassed Elliott at the restaurant by refusing his gift and walking out on him. I didn't raise you to be rude and insulting to someone who has been so nice to you."

Georgia's jaw nearly dropped at the accusation. As soon as her initial shock wore off, she folded her hands on the table and calmly addressed her mother, which took effort. "I refused his gift because it's too personal and intimate, and I didn't want that gift to come with any strings attached, or expectations."

Her mother scoffed. "That's ridiculous."

"No, it's not," Georgia refuted firmly. "Elliott has been under the impression that he and I are more than acquaintances, which we are not, and never have been. We've never formally dated, and I made it clear to him that I'm not interested in him at all. *You're* the one who's been pushing us together and leading him to believe we're such a great match, in hopes that I'll just fall in line like I normally do. And you need to know and hear me this time, that is not going to happen."

Her mother's gaze narrowed, anger flickering in the depths of her eyes. "I don't understand how you can be so ungrateful and selfish. We let you change your major, which upset your father so much he had a heart attack over the stress you put him through, and now this."

Georgia shook her head and laughed, though the sound lacked any humor. "I refuse to allow you to make me feel responsible for Dad's heart attack. I did not cause his health issues and blocked arteries because I made a decision that conflicted with *your* hopes and dreams. Ask his doctors if you don't believe me."

Her mother stiffened in her seat. "You didn't want to be a lawyer so you could one day take over the firm that's been in the family for three generations? Fine. But you could at least *try* to give Elliott a chance for the sake of the firm and the business your father and his father built. Elliott is already a junior partner, and your father has high hopes for him."

Of course her mother ignored the facts of what Georgia had said, instead focusing on her one and only goal. Anger surged through Georgia, and she tightened her already clasped hands on the table in an effort to maintain her composure.

"So let Dad give *Elliott* the business. It's not my responsibility to keep it in the family, and my private life is just that. *Private*, and I'd appreciate it if you'd stop meddling and interfering or telling me what to do." She drew a deep breath. "I'm an adult, I know my own mind, and I will never want to be in a relationship with Elliott."

Her mother's chin lifted. "I'm only doing what's best for the family and the business."

What was best for Nina Brooks, more likely.

And with that came the realization that she was

never going to change her mother's mind or get her to understand where Georgia was coming from or what she wanted in life. But she wasn't going to cave to her mother's expectations any longer, and she intended to make that crystal clear.

"Clearly, we're at an impasse." She stood up, because as soon as she had her say, she was leaving. She wouldn't keep rehashing this issue and argument with her mother. "I love you. I love Dad. And I'm not doing any of this to hurt you, but you need to understand things are going to be different from now on."

Her mother narrowed her gaze. "What does that mean?"

"It's simple. If I walk into a family dinner and you've invited Elliott...or any man as *my date*, I will leave. If I go to an event with you, and Elliott or anyone else just happens to be sitting at our table for my benefit, I won't stay. If I want to bring someone with me, that will be my choice and no one else's." Her insides trembled as she spoke, but she'd never been so certain of her words before.

The shock on her mother's face, along with the way her mouth gaped open, was almost comical. Georgia had only stood up to her parents once before when she'd been in college, but this moment was far more extreme. She'd just set definitive boundaries with her mother that came with consequences, and judging by the disapproval gradually transforming Nina's expression, she wasn't happy with Georgia's newly found confidence.

Once her mother recovered, she opened her mouth to speak, but Georgia held up a hand and cut her off before she could issue what would undoubtedly be a scathing reply.

"We're done with this conversation, Mom," she said firmly. "And I'm done with you manipulating my life. If you want a relationship where you make a genuine attempt to get to know me, then you know where to find me."

Then, she turned and walked out of the house, proud of herself for taking control of her life.

IT HAD BEEN one helluva long week for Drew, including working at the office on Saturday and tying up loose ends on an agreement between a client and the company they were purchasing. But Saturday evening was all about spending time with Georgia...especially when his boss had asked Drew for a firm decision next week on whether or not he'd accept the offer to head up the European deal.

Drew hadn't changed his mind and was still leaning toward saying yes. Passing up such a huge, lucrative opportunity wasn't in his nature. He wasn't about to settle for mediocrity in his career, and even though he'd recently made partner, he still had a lot to prove to the senior members of the firm. It was important to show he was a team player and could handle a client as important as EuroQuest Industries, which meant even longer hours at the office and a lot of traveling to Europe—especially during the initial months on the job.

The only difficulty in making the decision revolved around Georgia. He couldn't keep leading her on, and he was certain if his emotions were involved, which they were, then hers had to be, as well. Heartbreak was all but guaranteed. Selfishly, he wasn't ready to let her go just yet, which was why he'd agreed to whatever date she'd planned. Until he accepted that European offer, he was going to enjoy what little time they had left together.

After finishing at the office late Saturday afternoon, he made a quick stop at home to change into jeans and a more casual shirt, then picked up Georgia, who'd greeted him with a kiss and an exuberant hug. Her mood was directly related to the confrontation she'd had with her mother, one she'd told him about over the phone earlier in the week. She had a new, optimistic view of life and he loved seeing her recently discovered confidence. Her eyes sparkled, and her overall happy demeanor was infectious. It was obvious a huge weight had been lifted off her shoulders and her constant grin had Drew forgetting his own troubles for a while.

She kept their final destination a surprise, taking him first to eat at an Italian restaurant. Afterward, they arrived at the Vanderbilt Space Observatory and Planetarium on Long Island, leaving him in awe of how much thought she'd put into a date catered to his love of astronomy.

She'd already purchased tickets to the planetarium laser show, and after the event was over, they made their way up to the rooftop observatory to take in the clear night sky. Georgia enthusiastically pointed out all the constellations he'd taught her at the cabin, and even others that were more difficult to find.

He smiled, surprised and impressed by her expanded knowledge. "I see someone has been studying."

She laughed, the sound light and carefree. "I admit, I'm finding astronomy fascinating. I wouldn't have known about any of this if it wasn't for you. Now, when I look up at the night sky, I see it entirely differently."

He remembered feeling that same way after the first time his father had introduced him to the stars, and he'd learned about all the constellations.

She grabbed his hand and pulled him toward one of the higher-powered telescopes, where they were able to view the moon and some planets, including Jupiter, Saturn, and Venus. Based on her excitement, her interest in the solar system was genuine, and he enjoyed having a partner who liked the same things he did. It was a fun evening, and one he knew he'd never forget because that shared passion made him feel even more connected to her.

They spent over an hour finding different aspects of the planetary system together, and just when he thought they were done for the evening, Georgia withdrew an envelope from her purse.

"I have something special for you," she said, holding the item to him.

He took the envelope and tipped his head curiously at her. "What's this for?"

"It's a little thank you," she said softly. "For reminding me who I can be when I just trust myself and stick to my convictions."

He knew she was referring to the difficult conversation she'd finally had with her mother. "You don't need to thank me for that."

"I *wanted* to do this for you," she insisted, her eyes glimmering with excitement. "Go ahead. Open it up."

So, he did, withdrawing a parchment paper with the words "Certificate of Registration" at the top. Unsure of what he was looking at, he kept reading the typed words: *Let it be known that the star residing at the astronomically verified coordinates of RA 12.390 and Declination -2.57 is now hereby named WHITNEY DANIELS.*

He stared at the certificate, stunned by the realization that she'd named a star after his sister, and there wasn't a damn thing Drew could do about the emotion that tightened in his throat. Georgia's gift was so special and meaningful—not just because she'd tapped into his love of astronomy, which most people tended to find boring, but because she'd honored Whitney's memory in an unforgettable way she knew he'd love and appreciate. It was the most thoughtful thing he'd ever received.

He lifted his gaze back to her smiling face. He

didn't care whether or not they were alone. He pulled Georgia into his arms and hugged her tight. "Thank you," he said, his voice gruff with appreciation, and so much more. "This is amazing." *She* was amazing.

"You're welcome," she whispered. "Whitney deserves her own shining star."

He couldn't agree more, and he couldn't wait to share this with his family.

When he finally released her, she had her cell phone in her hand, and she opened up an app. "Let's find Whitney's star through the telescope. I just need the coordinates, and then we can search the sky once we see where it's located."

He gave her the information off the paper, which directed them to a bright star near Ursa Major. It took a bit of exploring, but they finally narrowed in on Whitney's star.

It was an extraordinary moment, and the emotion stayed with him during the ride home. When they arrived at her door, he gave her a soft, chaste kiss on the lips. One he swore was meant to show his gratitude and nothing more. Though he wanted to carry her inside and make love to her until the sun rose in the sky, he had no intention of following through on his desire. Knowing he was going to accept a job offer that would force him to end things between them, he had no right sleeping with her again. He couldn't have both the career and Georgia, and the time had come to begin that painful separation.

But his light kiss didn't stay sweet for long. A ravenous need for one more night had him lifting his hands to her face and tipping her head to the side to deepen the connection. She moaned against his lips, encouraging him with the touch and slide of her tongue against his, her fingers digging sharply into his shoulders as she clung to him, melting in his arms so perfectly.

Needing Georgia was like a fever in his blood, and it was so easy to ignore the reasons why this was a bad idea. Getting lost in *her* was the only thing that mattered. An overwhelming, desperate need pounded through him, and he picked her up and carried her to her bedroom before he could come to his senses, do the right thing, and walk away before things went any further.

Their clothes were quickly removed, and tonight, it wasn't just about giving and taking physical pleasure but imprinting everything about her in his mind and soul so he could take part of her with him. One last heated memory for all those cold, lonely nights ahead without her.

Pressing her back onto the mattress, he worshipped every inch of her body with his mouth and hands, until she was quivering on the brink of orgasm and shamelessly begging him to take her. His cock pulsed almost painfully, the need to be inside her so agonizing that he finally moved over her and settled between her spread legs, where he belonged.

He braced his forearms on the bed beside her and tangled his fingers in her silky hair. Gripping the strands tight, he tipped her head back, watching as her lips parted on a soft moan and her lashes fluttered closed as she waited for him to thrust inside her.

"Look at me, Georgia," he demanded gruffly.

Her eyes locked on his as he flexed his hips and pushed in, so slow he was aware of every inch she took of his cock and the slick, wet heat enveloping him. As much as he wanted to unleash his restraint and rut into her like an uncivilized caveman, he purposely kept things slow. Stretching out the pleasure. Savoring every sensation. Memorizing every sensual sound that slipped past her lips. As he bottomed out inside her, she whispered his name, then trembled as he gradually withdrew and clenched around his cock when he glided back in.

She let him make love to her at his leisure, giving him everything, open and vulnerable to him, both physically and emotionally. He saw it all in her eyes, felt it in the way her hands caressed his body, and how her legs wrapped around his waist, allowing him to penetrate as deep as possible.

He dipped his head and brushed his lips across her cheek, drifting down to her mouth so that he could kiss her, as slow and deep as his cock shuttling in and out of her. As the tension and friction between them increased, she made an impatient, mewling sound against his lips, arching beneath him while her hands drifted down to palm his ass and pull him closer, causing him to grind against her clit.

Her thighs clenched around his hips, and her body

writhed and shuddered beneath him as she chased the blissful pleasure beckoning, while his own desperate hunger coiled tighter inside him. Finally, she threw her head back with a soft cry, and he felt the rippling sensations along his cock as she came, her internal muscles gripping and stroking his shaft until he exploded in a hot rush inside her.

He buried his face against the fragrant curve of her neck, groaning long and low, the intensity of his climax completely overwhelming him.

Sex had never been like this before, stripped down to the basic human need to *connect* with a woman on a deeper, more intimate, and vulnerable level. Where pleasure was no longer the ultimate goal, but their connection was. Because they were so intrinsically linked, it was impossible not to feel every heartbeat between them.

Georgia had changed him in irrevocable ways. She'd filled parts of him he hadn't even known were missing, and in that moment, Drew knew without a doubt that he'd fallen in love with Georgia Brooks…and there wasn't a damn thing he could do about it.

Chapter Fourteen

G EORGIA LEFT WORK early Monday afternoon and headed to her father's office. She'd called earlier and talked to his secretary, Cynthia, who'd assured Georgia her father did not have any important meetings or scheduled calls. She wanted to catch him at work so she didn't have to head to the house and deal with her mother again since, as expected, Nina was still giving her the silent treatment after their conversation. She'd asked Cynthia to let her father know to expect her around four in the afternoon.

Georgia drove to the firm's building and tried not to think about Saturday night with Drew, since the evening had already consumed most of her thoughts for the day. Of course, she was unsuccessful. Together, they'd shared a perfect evening at the observatory, and an even better night when they'd returned to her apartment. The sex between them had been markedly different, more intimate, with an emotional component she'd felt to the depths of her soul.

That's why she'd been so confused when, after, he'd grown quiet and distant, withdrawing from her in an obvious way. The abrupt change in his personality had her thinking maybe their expiration date had arrived. They were only supposed to have her birthday weekend together. He'd agreed to prolong their time together and try for something more, but maybe she'd gotten too deep with the star she'd bought in his sister's name. Their lovemaking had been just that, and he'd clearly realized he wasn't ready for an exclusive relationship after all.

He hadn't said those words, though. In fact, when she'd asked if he was okay as she walked him to the door, he'd told her that he needed to figure a few things out, and they'd talk soon.

What the hell did that mean, anyway?

His unexpected shift in demeanor concerned her, but right now, she needed to resolve things with her father. Then she'd find out what was wrong with Drew. It would either be something they'd figure out together, or a decision he'd come to on his own, and it was a done deal. Either way, she needed answers.

Arriving at her father's building, she parked her car and rode the elevator up to his floor. The elevator opened up to a lobby area, and the young woman sitting behind the desk was obviously expecting her. As soon as Jolie saw her, the friendly receptionist smiled and told her to go back, her father was waiting for her.

Georgia made her way through workstations and other offices. As she walked past the legal library and research area, an open space with bookshelves and tables and chairs, she caught sight of Elliott, who glanced up from the hardbound book he was skimming through.

He frowned upon seeing her. There was no mistaking the bitterness in his expression as he watched her stroll by, but Elliott's mood wasn't her problem, and she ignored him. She had more pressing matters than Elliott's hurt feelings. It wasn't like she'd led him on in any way.

When she arrived at Cynthia's desk—the gatekeeper to her father's inner sanctum—the other woman gave her an amicable smile. "Hi, Georgia. Go on in. He's waiting for you."

"Thank you." She entered her father's office, and the familiar, comforting scent of leather and musk and his cologne filled her senses.

He stood up, came around his desk, and greeted her with a warm hug. The kind of embrace that was the complete opposite of her mother's detached and indifferent air kisses. It had always been that way. Warm versus cool.

"Well, this is a nice surprise," her father said, taking her elbow and guiding her to one of the leather seats in front of his desk.

She sat down, giving her father a wry smile and calling him out on his comment. "Is it *really* a surprise to see me?"

He chuckled and settled into the chair next to hers, instead of back behind his desk, which she appreciated. "I'll admit I've been waiting for you to either call or stop by when you were ready to speak to me. Your mother told me all about your visit on Friday, though I'm sure her version of events was very one-sided and skewed to make her look like the victim."

She blinked at him, startled by that statement coming from her father.

"Oh, come on, Georgia-Girl," he said, using the nickname he'd given her as a child, his tone affectionate. "Don't look so shocked. I know who your mother is. She'll never admit that anything is her fault, so why don't you tell me your side of things?"

Georgia wasn't sure what to make of her father's calm, rational response. She'd come to his office expecting to have to defend herself from whatever accusations her mother had made against her. Instead, her father was giving her the opportunity to speak without judgment.

"Did you have anything to do with wanting to set me up with Elliott?" she asked. "I mean, did you expect I'd just go along with things to make you and Mom happy?" She needed to know her father's role in things.

He shifted in his seat, obviously uncomfortable. "Well, you hadn't dated anyone in a while, so yes, I was the one who mentioned the idea to your mother, thinking how great it would be if you and Elliott hit it off and things worked out in a way that allowed the firm to stay in the family. But I never expected you to do something you didn't want to do just to please us. It's your mother who took the ball and ran with it, so to speak."

"That's one way of putting it," she muttered. "Mother laid the guilt and manipulation on pretty thick, and even reminded me of the heart attack and triple bypass you had after I made the decision to switch majors in college and not go to law school."

He looked appalled that Nina had blamed Georgia for his health issues. Finally, he shook his head. "I can't deny that your choice disappointed me, but you changing majors had nothing to do with me having a heart attack." He let out a long groan. "As for Elliott, I never thought your mother would take things so far. Apparently she was operating behind my back, more determined than even I realized to get you two together."

Georgia nodded, relieved to know her father hadn't been manipulating her too. She crossed her legs and exhaled a deep breath. "I went to see her on Friday to set things straight, and I guess I'm here to do the same with you."

He held up his hands, palms out. "There's nothing to set straight, Georgia. It's your life, your decision, and I respect that. Of course, I'd be lying if I didn't say I'd love for this firm to somehow stay in the family, but that's not your burden to carry." He lifted one shoulder and shrugged. "As it turns out, one of the senior partners has mentioned he's interested in buying me out when I'm ready to retire, so that's always an option."

"Just not one that makes Mom happy," I pointed out.

"No, but what matters most to me is *your* happiness, Georgia." He reached out and took the hand she had resting on the arm of the chair, giving it a gentle squeeze. "I would never want you to do anything that would make you miserable, or expect you to do something out of some sort of obligation or expectation. And I'm very sorry your mother doesn't feel the same way and has been torturing you over it. But I am very proud of you for not letting her walk all over you."

The apology in her father's voice was genuine, and it was at times like these that her parents seemed so mismatched in their priorities. As an attorney, her father had a strong, tenacious personality, and he didn't suffer fools, yet at home, he didn't always call his wife on her behavior…maybe to avoid an argument or confrontation? Georgia didn't know.

She didn't understand most of the dynamic between her parents, and it wasn't her place to analyze their marriage, or even question it. But there was one thing Georgia had realized. Her mother wasn't truly happy. Her husband gave her everything she wanted…except his time and attention. And those tangible things didn't make up for the lack of emotional connection, and Georgia had to wonder if her mother was trying to find her own happiness living through and at the expense of others.

"Elliott mentioned that you might be seeing Drew Daniels," her father said, pulling Georgia out of her thoughts.

Georgia was no longer shocked that Elliott had leaked that bit of information to her father. She didn't like the man at all, and still didn't know what her father saw in him, but her dad had the right to hire whoever he wanted. It wasn't Georgia's decision, and now that she'd put clear-cut boundaries between herself and Elliott, she no longer cared.

"I take it you know who he is?" she asked, since her father said Drew's name with such familiarity.

He laughed. "Of course I do. He's got quite an impressive reputation as a merger and acquisition attorney. His firm and ours were in negotiations with a company looking for a legal team to represent them in an eight-billion-dollar merger. They chose Drew's proposal over Elliott's, so he essentially stole the deal right out from under Elliott."

Georgia frowned. "Stole it?"

"Oh, it was all legal, of course," he said with a wave of his hand. "But it was a huge loss for our firm and for Elliott, who took it pretty badly. It's kind of hard to forget a loss like that one, not to mention the man savvy enough to pull it off."

Georgia found that bit of information enlightening. It certainly explained some of Elliott's jealousy and pettiness toward Drew.

After her conversation with her father, Georgia walked out of his office, only to be stopped by Elliott. He'd stepped out of a conference room and blocked her way.

"Excuse me," she said in a terse tone, expecting

him to move.

He didn't. Instead, he stepped closer, unmistakable resentment narrowing his eyes. Any niceties or pleasantries that might have existed between them, even if only on a surface level, were gone.

The corner of his mouth turned up in a cruel smile. "You do realize that the only reason Drew Daniels is dating you is to get back at me, don't you?"

Georgia rolled her eyes at his outrageous claim. "Whatever you say," she said, refusing to get into any argument. They were alone for the moment, but she had no desire to make a scene in her father's firm.

Even knowing the source of Elliott's grudge with Drew, she didn't believe for a second *Drew* was using her. Being vindictive and vengeful wasn't in Drew's nature. Even when he'd known Elliott had been trying to pursue her, Drew had never bad-mouthed his colleague. Elliott was the one with the malicious, jealous attitude as he tried to make Drew look bad in her eyes, but that wasn't going to happen.

She lifted her chin. "I don't appreciate you harassing me. Please step out of my way so I can leave."

Still, Elliott didn't budge and continued his rant. "Drew doesn't want you, except maybe to fuck around with," he said with an awful sneer that sent chills down her spine. "Maybe I was just going about things the wrong way with you. If I'd known you were such a whore, I'd—"

Furious at his gall, Georgia cut off his words with a hard slap across the face, one that made his head snap to the side and her own palm sting from the force of her blow. Her handprint immediately bloomed bright red on his cheek, and when he glanced back at her, his eyes darkened with rage.

"*Bitch*," he hissed spitefully, his entire body tensing with fury.

For a moment, she thought Elliott was going to lunge, and she inhaled a deep breath, preparing to scream.

"Elliott!" Georgia's father's voice boomed loudly, and she and Elliott jumped at Roland's unexpected presence down the hall. "I've seen and heard enough! Don't you *ever* threaten my daughter again. Get in my office," her father ordered Elliott. "*Now*."

Elliott's anger quickly morphed into fear, his eyes wide, remorse all over his expression. No doubt, he'd just realized he'd put his career in jeopardy. Averting his gaze, he kept his mouth shut as he did as her father had ordered. Head down, he strode in the direction of his boss's office.

Georgia's father approached her, and she was suddenly aware that a few other employees had stepped out of their offices to see what was going on.

"Are you okay?" Her father placed his hands on Georgia's arms, his worried gaze scanning her face. "Did he touch you at all?"

She shook her head, still shaken by the whole incident. "No. I'm the one who slapped him because of what he said to me."

"He deserved it," her father growled protectively.

"I heard and saw it all. I promise you, this will *never* happen again. I don't employ people with volatile tempers and anger management issues, and clearly, that's the case with Elliott." He shook his head. "I don't know how I misjudged him for so long."

"Ambitious people know how to hide their true selves, Dad." Georgia didn't feel bad that Elliott had just gotten himself fired, considering he'd instigated the entire confrontation, the idiot. "Do you need me to stay?"

It was the last thing Georgia wanted to do, but she wasn't sure if her father needed a statement from her for human resources to back up his decision to terminate Elliott's employment.

Her father pulled her into his warm embrace and kissed her temple. "No. You can go. I'll take care of things." He released her and stepped back, his expression apologetic. "And again, I'm sorry."

She nodded, appreciating her father's kindness and caring. If it were her mother in this situation, Georgia was fairly certain she would have made excuses for Elliott's reprehensible behavior.

She said goodbye to her father, and headed for the parking garage.

At least she'd never have to face Elliott again. The knots in her stomach eased as she slid into her car and exhaled a deep breath to calm her frazzled nerves.

Closing her eyes, she recounted her successes. She'd talked to her mother, resolved things with her father, and now there was only one person left she needed to speak to. Drew.

She didn't believe a word Elliott had said about him, but considering what she'd just gone through with Elliott, she wanted to hear Drew's side of their history and obvious one-sided rivalry. Then, she needed to talk to Drew about something even more important. Them.

Georgia wasn't a casual dater or someone who could handle a "friends with benefits" type arrangement. Not when her heart was involved. And it was. Very deeply. As difficult as it would be to walk away from him, she couldn't keep seeing him without the security of knowing they were headed toward something more meaningful.

She *deserved* a commitment and the reassurance that he was in this relationship as deeply as she was. Right now, she was in a place of limbo, and she needed answers, even if they weren't the ones she wanted to hear.

She pulled her phone from her purse and sent him a text: **I'd like to speak to you in person. Can I come over to your place when you get home from work?**

His response came shortly after: **Yes. I'll be home by seven. I need to talk to you, as well.**

And there it was, she thought with a sinking feeling in her stomach. *The dreaded talk.* The beginning of the end. There was no other reason she could think of that he'd need to speak with her. Not after how withdrawn and distant he'd been when he'd left her Saturday night.

His behavior had been a warning, and as much as she wanted to fight for their relationship, she couldn't do that if it was all one-sided. But she intended to give it her best shot.

Chapter Fifteen

D REW PACED THE living room of his apartment as he waited for Georgia to arrive, his own anxiety and dread over their upcoming conversation eating away at him…along with the guilt he'd been carrying since leaving her place Saturday night.

If he were honest with himself, this difficult discussion should have happened then, but telling Georgia they were over felt like a shitty thing to do after the special evening they'd shared. She'd given him one of the most memorable nights of his adult life and walking away from it and her was so fucking hard.

But he owed her the truth before tomorrow morning when he would agree to manage the EuroQuest Industries contract. He couldn't keep stringing her along with the hope that one day he would have time for *them*. It wasn't fair to expect her to be a part-time girlfriend, available on his schedule. He couldn't guarantee any kind of consistency. Couldn't make any promises and would probably, in fact, break more than he kept. That kind of unpredictability wasn't fair. His ex-girlfriend could fill Georgia in on the kind of life she'd have with him and he already knew the loneliness wouldn't make her happy. Georgia deserved better.

But all those valid reasons did nothing to alleviate the ache in his chest. Or soothe his heart that already felt like it was breaking in two at the thought of letting go of the one woman who'd given him so much, and who made him feel so whole and complete. Georgia had seen sides to him he'd never been comfortable sharing with any other woman, and imagining his life without her in it was excruciatingly painful.

She arrived a short while later, and he let her into his apartment. Normally, he'd pull her into his arms and kiss her, and he had to physically resist the instinctive urge to do so now. To hug her would only send mixed signals and messages. Besides, her own tense body language told him in no uncertain terms, *don't touch*.

He wasn't used to her being aloof, and no matter how much he deserved this cool attitude after how he'd left last time, it stung.

"Hey," he said, forcing a smile. "Come on in. Can I get you something to drink?" he asked, feeling fucking awkward. Something else he'd never experienced around Georgia.

"No, thank you." Her tone and demeanor were guarded.

With nothing left to do, he led the way into the living room, where she settled in a single armchair. He chose the sofa across from her. Distance that hurt.

"You said you needed to talk to me about something, so you can go first," he offered, telling himself he was acting like a gentleman when he was just being a goddamn coward and delaying the inevitable.

She blew out a soft breath. "Okay, so first, I wanted to talk to you about Elliott."

He was thrown off by her choice of subject matter. "What about him?" he asked.

She crossed one leg over the other, and since she was wearing a skirt and high heels, he was momentarily distracted by those long, toned, sexy limbs. Until she spoke, redirecting his attention back up to her face—that at the moment, wasn't giving much of her feelings away.

"I went to my father's office earlier today. He and I needed to settle things after the whole *Elliott and my mother* situation. As I walked out, Elliott confronted me in the hallway."

Drew's entire body tensed. "Confronted you...how?"

She drew a deep breath. "He made a snide remark about how you're just using me to get back at him," she said, and before he could refute that claim in any way, she held up a hand to stop him. "I don't believe that for a second, but it's been clear since the beginning that there is some kind of rivalry between you two."

"Jesus Christ," he muttered in annoyance. "Any rivalry is all one-sided because Elliott is an insecure little weasel."

She smirked. "I would agree with that assessment,"

she said, but her expression quickly turned serious. "He then went on to say some very derogatory, threatening things."

Drew gripped the edge of the sofa tighter in one hand. "Such as?"

An embarrassed flush stained her cheeks, and he knew he wouldn't like what she said next. "Like he was going about things with me the wrong way and that maybe he needed to treat me like a whore instead."

The fury that surged through Drew's bloodstream was insane, and he curled both hands into fists at his sides. "I'm going to kill that fucker the next time I see him."

She shook her head. "No need to get your hands dirty," she said, a small smile tugging at her lips, confusing him until she said, "I slapped him for the vulgar comment, hard enough that he probably saw stars."

Drew couldn't help but grin with relief, and pride. "That's my girl," he said, the praise automatic, even if she wasn't going to be his for long.

That pink flush staining her cheeks deepened because she *liked* getting his approval. And man, that did something for him.

Her voice cut into his thoughts.

"Apparently, my father heard everything Elliott said to me, and he was livid. I'm sure that by now, Elliott is unemployed. But regardless, I just want to hear your side of the story. All of it, so I understand his jealousy and rage."

Drew swallowed back a groan. That dick was the last thing he wanted to talk about, but considering what the bastard had said to Georgia about Drew using her to get back at him, she deserved to know their history.

"It's pretty simple. We went to law school together," he said, sitting forward on the couch and bracing his arms on his thighs. "I was always top of the class, and Elliot…was not. I was head of the law review magazine, I passed the bar exam the first time. I always edged him out, not because I was trying to be competitive with him, but because I worked my ass off for *me*. And since he was an insecure and jealous little fucker, he resented the fact that I was flat out better than him."

"I can believe that," she murmured.

"So, he instigated a rivalry, which truly was one-sided because I didn't have to prove shit to him to be successful. Hell, he wasn't ever on my radar. But his snide remarks continued through law school. Once we graduated, I thought that would be the end of seeing him again, but we both applied to McKenzie Goodwin because they're one of the most prestigious and reputable corporate law firms in New York City. I was hired, and Elliott wasn't, which made him even more spiteful, even though he was hired on at your father's firm shortly after." Drew shook his head at the stupidity of it all. "It was all really childish if you ask me."

Georgia arched a brow at him. "I suppose it didn't help matters that a proposal you put together led to

McKenzie Goodwin being awarded representation for an eight-billion-dollar merger over Elliott's proposal from my father's firm."

"How did you know about that?" he asked, surprised.

"My father told me." Her smile softened her features. "I think he was secretly impressed by you."

Drew shrugged. "Clearly, our proposal was what the company was looking for. But that loss pulled the rug out from under Elliott for the second time, in a big way. Especially since he lost the deal to *me*. Shortly after that, I made partner while he waited another year, and for someone who is so competitive, I'm sure the whole thing chafed."

"I'm sure it did," she murmured in reply.

He exhaled a deep breath. "So, when Elliott saw us together when he clearly wanted you for himself, it had to drive him insane to think you chose me over him."

"Which now all makes sense," she said, smoothing a hand down the front of her skirt, her gaze holding his. "Thank you for telling me all that. Why didn't you mention it before? I know I asked."

"Because I didn't want to waste our valuable time together talking about that asshole."

Her grin told him she understood.

The living room then grew quiet for an uncomfortable span of time before Georgia spoke again. "You said there was something you needed to talk to me about?"

He scrubbed a hand along his jaw, his chest already becoming uncomfortably tight. Doing the right thing had never felt so fucking *wrong*, and it took effort to start this conversation. "I do. Tomorrow I have a meeting with my boss that is going to change things for me."

She tipped her head to the side, her expression unreadable, making it difficult to gauge her emotions, which he hated when she was usually such an open book.

"How so?" she asked, clutching her hands together in her lap.

He held her gaze and pushed through. "I'm accepting an offer to head the legal team representing a new corporation we just signed. It's a massive deal and a huge boon for my career. It's going to consume most of my time, and I'll be traveling to Europe often in the next six months."

"Congratulations. That's really fantastic." She smiled at him, but it didn't reach her eyes because she was smart and knew he had more to say and was clearly anticipating what was coming.

Fuck, he did *not* want to do this, but he had no choice. He forced out the words stuck in his throat. "I think it would be best if we...ended things."

"Of course you do," she said softly. And since Georgia wasn't the type of woman to yell, scream, or cry, her eyes merely flashed with a gut-wrenching pain he felt all the way to his soul. "So, that's it?" she asked. "We're just done?"

"I won't have the time for us," he said, his voice sounding as rough as sandpaper to his own ears. "The hours involved in this negotiation, the frequent travel…it's going to be an insane schedule for quite a while, and I'll have little to no time left over."

Her lips pursed. "So you've taken it upon yourself to make the decision for both of us? Without asking how I feel about the new challenges in your life?"

The hurt in her voice cut through him like a knife. "I don't have to ask because I already know how a relationship under these circumstances would turn out."

She narrowed her gaze. "How could you possibly know that?"

He blew out a harsh breath. "Because I've been in this situation before, and it did not end well."

She stared at him, clearly confused by his comment because he'd never told her about Angie.

"My last serious relationship ended because she felt I wasn't present in the relationship. My ex was lonely and slept with another man because she felt neglected, and that was *before* I made partner at the firm. Now, I'm going to be five times busier once I accept this offer, with very little quality time left to nurture a relationship with you."

She stared as he spoke, not interrupting. He had no idea what she was thinking, and he ran a hand through his hair in frustration. "Look, I'm trying to do the right thing because I never want you to end up resenting me because I can't give you what you need.

What you *deserve*." He needed her to understand where he was coming from and see he was doing what was best. Even if it hurt like hell.

The sadness in her eyes was killing him and when she finally spoke, she pushed the knife in further. "Do you realize you never asked me what *I* needed in a relationship? Instead, you made your decision based on another woman who did a shitty thing and hurt you. It's like you don't know me, and by now, you really should." She shook her head sadly.

"Georgia—"

"No. It's my turn to speak. During our time together, I've proven I know, value, *and love* everything about the dedicated, loyal man you are."

His heart stopped in his chest at her declaration and scrambled his brain, which gave her time to stand up and approach him, clearly not finished having *her* say. He rose to his feet but remained silent.

"You should have asked my opinion about *us*. Instead, you just decided it was best to end things. Your choice, your decision. And if that's what you really want, fine. I don't need a man in my life who doesn't love and want me the way I do him."

He opened his mouth, though he had no idea what he wanted to say, and she held up her hand again. Having learned his lesson, he shut it and let her continue.

"Before I leave, I want you to know something. I'd never expect more than you could give. I know what I'm getting into with an attorney. I grew up with a

CARLY PHILLIPS & ERIKA WILDE

father in this field, and I know the commitment it takes to be successful as a lawyer, that there will be times when things get canceled or cases come up that consume all of your time. But you know what?" she asked, and he knew she didn't expect him to respond.

"I'm an independent woman," she went on, her shoulders straightening. "I have a job that I love, which…surprise!…sometimes demands more than just normal nine-to-five hours. I have my own friends I like to spend time with, so while you're busy at work or out of the country, I'd be just fine. We went all last week without seeing each other, and guess what? I didn't fall apart. I never once felt neglected or ignored because we found other ways to still *be present* in each other's lives. Texts, phone calls, and a quick FaceTime work, you know? I missed you, but I was willing to do whatever it takes to make a relationship between us work…because I love you," she said, her voice tangled with emotion.

His logical brain searched for a way to counter everything she'd said and fell short, and the words *I love you* remained lodged in his throat, pure fear consuming him. "Georgia—"

She shook her head. "And by the way, the only thing I *need and deserve* is a man who trusts me and believes we can make this work. Everything else would have fallen into place. And without it, well, we don't have much of a foundation, do we?"

It was a rhetorical question, a statement that felt like a hard punch to his gut. She'd called him out, and she was right. He'd been so caught up in *doing the right thing*, that he'd failed to take all those other important details into consideration.

With all the incredible strength and confidence she'd found within herself the past few weeks, she gave him one last sad smile, then turned and walked to the door.

He watched her leave, a cold, hard knot of dread in his stomach. A voice screamed in his head, *Don't let her go, don't fucking let her go...*but he stood there, watching her leave. And when the door shut behind her, the quiet solitude that surrounded him was nearly suffocating.

What the fuck did he just do?

Chapter Sixteen

THE MOMENT GEORGIA walked out the door, Drew knew he'd made a huge fucking mistake. He poured way too much bourbon into a glass and sat down in the chair Georgia had occupied earlier, intent on letting the alcohol dull the pain in his heart and calm the chaos in his head.

The regret nearly choking him was overwhelming, and he felt torn in two different directions—between a career he'd worked so hard to build for himself, and the woman he loved. And he did love Georgia, in ways that he'd never, ever loved another woman. He thought he'd made the right decision to sever things, but considering everything she'd said, he'd royally fucked up.

He took a generous gulp of bourbon, relishing the burn as he swallowed. Gradually, with every drink of the liquor, the misery swirling inside of him dimmed to a blunt ache that allowed his swirling confusion to calm.

Exhaling a deep breath, Drew leaned his head back on the edge of the chair and closed his eyes. He could now process everything that Georgia had said to him without feeling as though his heart was being ripped out of his chest, and one thing became crystal clear. Georgia wasn't Angie. Drew had been so hung up on the past he'd projected those fears onto his relationship with Georgia, assuming she'd come to resent him and his job.

But the biggest difference between Angie and Georgia was that deep, emotional connection he'd formed with Georgia, which was why the moment she walked out the door he felt as though his entire world had just been flipped upside down and inside out. Like he'd never be able to be whole and complete again. Just like taking his next breath, he *needed* Georgia in his life.

The hard truth of the matter was, he hadn't been present in Angie's life because he hadn't been emotionally invested in *them*. Whereas, now that he had his blinders off, he could easily see himself married to Georgia, having a family with her, growing old with her…

His brother Beck's voice sounded in his head, along with the one piece of advice he'd given Drew when they'd met for dinner at The Back Door and discussed Georgia. *It all depends on how much you're willing to sacrifice to be with her.*

His brother would call him a dumbass for letting her go. Creating a stable, lasting relationship was all about sacrifices, and he *finally* knew he was willing to make those compromises happen to be with Georgia. There was no reason he couldn't have it all, just like

she'd told him. She was the one woman who compli-
mented him so perfectly, and was absolutely
irreplaceable. Without a doubt, he knew she was worth
fighting for, every single day of his life.

But before he made those promises to Georgia, he
needed to sober up for such an incredibly important
conversation, and he also needed to settle things at
work so he could give her the commitment she
deserved.

DESPITE HIS FAINT hangover, Drew strode into work
the following morning, no regrets lingering about his
decision. When the meeting with his boss rolled
around at ten, Drew entered Gregory's office with the
same determination and confidence he used to seal any
multimillion-dollar deal.

They discussed a few client contracts they were
working on before Gregory finally got down to the
business Drew had been waiting for.

His boss leaned forward in his leather seat and
clasped his hands on the desk. "So, the senior members and I are hopeful that you've made the decision
to head up the legal team for EuroQuest," he said.

He drew a long breath and spoke. "I gratefully accept," he told his mentor.

Gregory rose to his feet and when Drew did the
same, they shook hands, a pleased smile on the older
man's face. "I am thrilled," he said. "I wanted the best

person for the job on this project, and you're it."

"I appreciate your faith in me," Drew said. "It has been an insane twenty-four hours while coming to a final decision," he admitted.

"Do you mind if I ask why? I'd think this opportunity was everything you've been working toward."

"And you'd be correct." Drew managed a wry smile. "But it seems there's this woman…"

He went on to tell his mentor about Georgia, how much she meant to him, how he saw a potential forever future with her. And because Gregory had always been like a second father to him, especially when Drew's own dad had been so sick with cancer, he explained all the stupid, idiotic things he'd said to Georgia last night.

"Honestly, I was letting the past consume me, and I didn't give her enough credit." His smile widened at the thought of her dictating to him how independent she was, how disappointed she'd been that he'd tried to make decisions for her.

He wouldn't make that mistake again.

Gregory chuckled. "She sounds perfect for you. Much like my Diana is for me. Drew, nobody ever said you had to choose between your career here and your personal life. Look around you. Many partners in the firm are married, have children, take vacations, and enjoy life. Do we work more hours than most?" He nodded. "Of course we do because that's the nature of this business. But it sounds like you have the right woman in your corner."

Drew winced, hoping like hell he hadn't burned a bridge he'd never be able to repair. "About that. I haven't made things right yet."

"Then I suggest you do," Gregory encouraged him with a knowing look. "Before I let the partners know your decision and work piles up on your desk. You'll have to choose your team for this project."

He nodded gratefully. "I will. Thank you for believing in me."

Gregory shook his hand again. "You've earned it. Now go figure out the most important part of being the man in a relationship."

"What would that be?" Drew asked curiously.

"The art of a good grovel."

GEORGIA OPENED HER door to her sister holding a bottle of wine and a carton of chocolate chip ice cream.

Courtney gave her a commiserating smile. "I'm so sorry things didn't work out with Drew. I know it's not even noon, but which will it be to drown your sorrows? Wine or ice cream?"

Somehow, Georgia managed a laugh, appreciating her sister's support and humor. After calling into work this morning and taking a personal day off to mope over her break up with Drew—a girl was allowed at least one day to do so, in her opinion—she'd texted her sister with the news. Leave it to Courtney to show up with alcohol and sugar to distract her from her broken heart.

Georgia stepped back to let her sister inside. "I think I'll take both."

Courtney laughed as she headed for the kitchen, with Georgia following behind. "Hey, this is a judgment-free zone, except pardon me for saying so, but you look like hell."

Honestly, Georgia felt like hell, as though she was dealing with an emotional hangover after last night's conversation with Drew. She had zero makeup on, and her eyes were puffy from the few times she'd allowed herself a good cry. Her hair was a disheveled mess since she hadn't brushed it after waking up, and she was still wearing her pajamas—an old pair from college with cute little corgis and hearts on the shirt and shorts. The print was faded, the fabric well worn, but the set was what she considered her comfort pajamas and was appropriate for her pity party. Her sister was lucky she'd at least brushed her teeth.

She leaned against the counter while her sister poured two glasses of the moscato, then handed one to Georgia. "I figure since this is my one day to feel sorry for myself and wallow in self-pity that I'd go all out."

Courtney's gaze softened. "Fair enough."

Her sister scooped a bowl full of ice cream, handed it to Georgia with a spoon, and the two of them went back to the living room. Georgia curled up at the far end of the sofa with a blanket and began eating her treat guilt-free while Courtney settled on the other end.

Her sister let her enjoy a few bites of the ice cream before asking, "How are you doing, Georgie? Seriously."

She shrugged. "Not great at the moment, but I'll survive."

She went on to tell Courtney about the conversation she and Drew had had the previous night. The things she'd said, their discussion about his rivalry with Elliott, and the other surprising thing he'd told her about his ex, Angie, which had taken Georgia completely by surprise.

"A part of me can understand why Drew is wary about making a commitment after being hurt like that, but it would have been nice if I'd known what he'd been through before, so we could have discussed *our* relationship, instead of him making the decision to end things because *he* felt it was the right thing to do. That's the part that hurts the most."

"He's a man," Courtney said with a roll of her eyes as she took a drink of her wine. "They don't like to spew their emotions."

Georgia winced. "Well, I spewed mine. I told him I loved him." And she had no regrets about revealing her feelings, even if she hadn't heard the words back.

Courtney's eyes widened. "And?"

Sighing, Georgia pushed the ice cream around in the bowl with her spoon. "In all honesty, I didn't give him much of a chance to respond since I was in the middle of my tirade about being an independent woman who didn't need to be coddled and all that. But he actually looked...anguished." And she couldn't forget that misery on his face.

Courtney swirled the last bit of moscato in her wineglass, thinking for a moment. "Maybe he feels the same way and couldn't bring himself to say it, thinking it would only complicate matters."

"Maybe," Georgia said in a quiet tone. "I'll never know, will I?"

She didn't want to keep rehashing those painful memories and instead asked Courtney about her latest project. Courtney told her about the gallery sales she'd made on a few pieces, and showed her photos of the whimsical owl she was currently sculpting.

A knock on the door startled them both, and they jumped.

"Are you expecting anyone?" Courtney asked.

Georgia shook her head. "No."

She moved to get up, but Courtney did so first, heading to the door to see who it was. When she opened it, Drew stood on the other side.

Georgia sucked in a startled breath, and her heart began beating wild and fast in her chest. He looked utterly gorgeous in a charcoal-gray tailored suit. His dark-brown hair was mussed, as if he'd been tunneling his fingers through the strands. For a man who was always so confident, he appeared...nervous, his forehead creased with apprehension.

"Hi, Courtney—"

Her bold-as-brass sister didn't let him finish. "I hope you're here to grovel," she said, poking her finger against his chest as she spoke. "Because if you're here for any other reason, or you hurt my sister any more than you already have, I'm going to make it *very* hard for you to walk the next time I see you. *Got it?*"

The corner of his mouth twitched, and he nodded succinctly. "Loud and clear."

"Good." Courtney let him in, then glanced at Georgia. "Do you want me to stay?"

Georgia stood up, because sitting with Drew still standing made her feel much too vulnerable. She had no idea why he was here, but she shored up that same determination and fortitude that had gotten her through last night, along with pulling her protective walls even higher.

"No, we'll be fine," she told Courtney.

Her sister walked back, grabbed her purse, and started for the door, stopping in front of Drew before leaving. She gave him another finger jab in his chest. "Don't fuck this up like you did last night!" she said, then stalked out the door, leaving them alone.

"She's such a charmer," Drew said. He moved into the living area, closer to Georgia, his gaze taking in her unkempt appearance from head to toe…and softening at what he saw.

Keeping her distance, Georgia crossed her arms over her chest defensively and lifted her chin. "She's just being…protective."

"I get why," he said, regret written on his face. "I said some incredibly stupid things last night, and I hurt you, badly. I'm sorry for that."

"Yes, you did." She had no idea where this was leading, but she refused to let him off the hook so quickly. "Is that what you're here for, to apologize? Because if so, apology accepted, and you can leave knowing your conscience is clear."

Georgia was shocked by the slow, sexy grin that spread across his lips. And even more startled by the way her traitorous body reacted to that sinful gesture.

"Damn, you're not going to make this easy on me, are you?" he said, shaking his head, an almost amused look on his face.

She shrugged as the smallest bit of hope blossomed in her. "I don't know what you mean."

"Oh, I think you do," he said, pushing his hands into the front pockets of his slacks. "You've accepted my apology, but you haven't forgiven me."

Oh, yeah, her heart was now ricocheting in her chest. "I didn't realize you were looking to be forgiven."

"The only way we're going to get past what happened last night and move forward is for me to earn your forgiveness for making the first of many mistakes in our relationship."

He was talking in the present tense, and it took everything in her not to fold like a house of cards. She'd gotten an apology, but she deserved to know what had changed since they'd parted ways the previous evening—and what would change going forward. "You can certainly try."

He nodded and exhaled a deep breath. "First of all, you were right. It was wrong of me to make a unilateral decision for us to break up. If we'd had that discussion and openly communicated, this never would have happened."

"Agreed," she said.

"But based on my past, I thought I was doing the right thing. I believed that I couldn't have a successful, insanely busy career *and* you, until you lit into me about how stupid and short-sighted I was being." He held her gaze, sincerity glimmering in the depths. "In that moment, I hated every word you said because I saw how badly I'd hurt you. But at the same time, the things you said were exactly what I needed to hear. I just didn't realize what a dipshit I'd been until you left."

"Yes, you were," she said, shifting on her bare feet, not quite ready to let him know that she'd already forgiven him. Whatever he had to say, she wanted to hear it all.

"I need a strong woman in my life to keep me in line. One who isn't afraid to kick my ass when I need it, like you did last night," he went on, his tone now a bit gruff. "I need *you* in my life because I can't imagine it without you."

A lump formed in her throat, tears burned her eyes, and she valiantly tried to blink them back. "Go on," she said in a raspy voice.

He chuckled, the sound tinged with relief, as if he knew he'd made it over the first hurdle of forgiveness.

"The most important thing is that I love you, Georgia Brooks, *everything* about you," he said, the declaration soft and low. "I love your smiles and optimism. I love how vulnerable you are with me. I love your caring side and that adorable scar on your chin and how everything is so perfect and right in my world with you in it. But just in case that's not enough to sway you...you're the only one for me, and for the rest of our lives, I will do whatever it takes for you to feel that, every single day."

Her shoulders slumped in relief. He'd given her everything she needed to hear and more to assure her he was in this for the long haul, and she finally put him out of his misery and moved toward him. He watched her approach, looking uncertain until she slid her arms around his waist and hugged him tight, leaning her head against his chest. With a groan of relief, he pulled her even closer, and she felt the tension leave his body and the steady beating of his heart against her ear.

"I take it you've forgiven me?" he whispered against her hair.

She lifted her head and looked into his eyes, smiling. "I forgave you a while ago, but I needed to hear everything you had to say. We're going to make mistakes, but I will *always* forgive you because I love you, and I can't imagine my life without you in it, either."

He lifted his hands, and framing her face in his

palms, he lowered his head and kissed her until she was breathless and ready to climb him like a tree.

After a while, he lifted his lips from hers, his gaze hooded as he stared down at her face. "So, I've got the rest of the day off…I think our first fight calls for an afternoon of hot, sweaty make-up sex, don't you?"

She laughed, not opposed to that idea, then remembered he'd had a meeting with his boss this morning. "First, what did you decide to do about the European offer?"

He grinned confidently. "I did the only thing I could do. I accepted because I want it all. My career *and* my girl."

"Good," she said, happy for him. "You made the right choice."

He smirked. "I'm just full of great choices today."

She rolled her eyes. "Maybe you're just full of—"

The last word left her on a squeal of surprise as he swept her into his arms and carried her toward her bedroom. "Watch your mouth, Ms. Brooks," he said in a sexy, playful drawl.

"Or what?" she retorted in a sassy reply.

He tossed her onto the bed and started stripping out of his clothes. "Or else I'll have to put it to better use."

She licked her lips as he unbuckled his belt, unzipped his pants, and shoved them down until his already erect cock sprang free. "I'd like to see you try," she taunted.

His smile was hot and wicked as he tangled his fingers in her hair, pulled her toward him, and did just that, putting her mouth to work in the most delightfully seductive way.

Epilogue

Six months later…

A FTER A WEEK in Europe hammering out the last of negotiations between EuroQuest and the corporation they'd purchased in a multi-billion-dollar deal, Drew was exhausted and happy to be on US soil again. A town car picked him up from the airport, and on the drive to his apartment he sent a text to Georgia to let her know he was home.

It was late Saturday afternoon, and all he wanted to do was see his girl, take a hot shower, eat dinner, and spend the rest of the evening getting even with Georgia for that sexy FaceTime call she'd teased him with a few nights ago. The one where she'd called him wearing that seductive lingerie she'd gotten for her birthday, including the crotchless panties, and she'd roleplayed being his own personal "cam girl." She'd been bold and uninhibited, and her sexual confidence as she touched herself while he watched was the hottest fucking thing. She loved being his bad girl.

Yeah, he'd gotten off on the roleplay, but jacking off with his hand was nothing compared to releasing inside Georgia's soft, warm body. And after a week of being gone, he had a whole lot of pent-up sexual tension to unleash on her.

They'd both made a concerted effort to keep that fire going, even while he was away. They also spoke on the phone every single day and texted throughout. No doubt, the time apart was difficult, but he'd never felt so connected to Georgia. Never had to worry that him being away was anything more than a physical separation because the emotional bond between them was just as solid and strong.

Two months ago, when her lease was up on her apartment, he'd asked her to move in with him. With both of their busy schedules and his long hours, he wanted as much time together as they could get...he wanted to always come home to her in the evenings and wake up with her in his arms. There was no need for them to live separately when he knew this was the woman he intended to spend his life with.

Now that he'd wrapped up the EuroQuest contract, he wouldn't be traveling as often for a while, and he needed to make a proposal happen.

He'd already gone to dinner with Georgia's parents a few times—initially, to introduce him as her boyfriend, which had included a cool and frosty introduction to Nina Brooks, but every time they'd gotten together since, he'd deliberately charmed her, and Georgia's mother seemed to thaw a bit more around him each time.

As for her dad, they hit it off famously, probably because they both worked in the same field of law and had so much in common. Roland had hinted a few times that he'd could use an attorney like Drew at his firm, but he'd made it clear he wasn't interested. He wasn't with Georgia to take over her father's law firm…he was happy exactly where he was.

The town car arrived at their building, and Drew headed up to their apartment and let himself inside, always in awe of how Georgia had made his once minimalist place a real home. Her taste in décor was exceptional, a perfect balance of warmth and soothing colors, comfortable furniture, and contemporary artwork that made him love each and every room she'd redesigned.

Georgia's favorite playlist of songs drifted out of the speakers in the living room, covering up any noise he might have made as he entered. She wasn't in any of the front rooms, so he set his suitcase down and shrugged out of the leather jacket he'd traveled in.

"Honey, I'm home!" he called out playfully.

He heard a squeal of excitement from one of the back rooms, then Georgia appeared in the hallway, running toward him with a huge, happy grin on her face, with her hair in a ponytail and those sexy yoga pants conforming to her curves. He knew what was coming and braced himself as she leaped into his arms, and he caught her with his hands under her ass as she wrapped her arms around his neck and her legs around his waist. He couldn't help but laugh at her enthusiasm as she kissed him all over his face.

"I'm so happy to have you back," she said, her lips finally meeting his. "I've missed you so much!"

She kissed him more deeply, and the contentment he felt with her was unmatched. It flowed through him, anchoring him in a way that felt like a lifeline. She was the only one he needed in his life, the only one he wanted to come home to every single day.

She ended the kiss, her soft sigh brushing across his lips.

"Marry me," he blurted out.

He felt her jolt in his arms, and her eyes went wide as she stared into his. "What?"

He winced at his clumsy and unplanned proposal. He knew she'd heard him, and this wasn't the way he'd imagined asking her… "Shit. I know I should have done this big, romantic thing, but—"

She clapped a hand over his mouth. "I don't need anything big or romantic. Yes, of course I'll marry you!"

He exhaled a relieved breath. "I'm sorry I don't have a ring." God, he felt like a doofus, but she laughed, clearly not angry.

"I'm not worried," she said wryly.

He grinned. "We'll have a huge engagement party, and I'll do whatever else you want to celebrate."

"I already have everything I want," she said, smiling at him with pure adoration. "I have you."

He pressed his forehead to hers, realizing just how lucky he was to have this woman as his own. "I love you, Georgia Brooks. You make everything seem possible."

She lightly kissed his lips again. "That's because it is."

Thanks for reading! Up next at the bachelor auction: Tripp Daniels in JUST A LITTLE PROMISE. (Beck Daniels' brother from JUST ONE SCANDAL by Carly Phillips).

Read the next Kingston ~ Dare story: Meet the last single Dare sibling standing, Zach Dare in JUST ONE TEASE.

Other books in the Dare Crossover Bachelor Auction Series:
JUST A LITTLE HOOKUP
JUST A LITTLE SECRET
JUST A LITTLE PROMISE

For Book News:
SIGN UP for Carly's Newsletter:
carlyphillips.com/CPNewsletter
SIGN UP for Erika's Newsletter:
geni.us/ErikaWildeNewsletter

Carly Phillips and Erika Wilde Booklist

A Dare Crossover Series
Just A Little Hookup
Just A Little Secret

Dirty Sexy Series
Dirty Sexy Saint
Dirty Sexy Inked
Dirty Sexy Cuffed
Dirty Sexy Sinner

Book Boyfriend Series
Big Shot
Faking It
Well Built
Rock Solid

The Boyfriend Experience

About the Authors

CARLY PHILLIPS is the bestselling author of over eighty sexy contemporary romances featuring hot men, strong women, and the emotionally compelling stories her readers have come to expect and love. She is happily married to her college sweetheart and the mother of two adult daughters and their crazy dogs. She loves social media and is always around to interact with her readers. You can find out more and get two free books at www.carlyphillips.com.

ERIKA WILDE is the author of the sexy Marriage Diaries series and The Players Club series. She lives in Oregon with her husband and two daughters, and when she's not writing you can find her exploring the beautiful Pacific Northwest. For more information on her upcoming releases, please visit website at www.erikawilde.com.

Made in United States
North Haven, CT
18 July 2023

39203322R00127